"Your Hands Are Cold,"

he said. "Don't you ever wear gloves, or have you lost them?"

She looked up into his deep blue eyes and was lost. "It's hard to make a checklist when I'm wearing gloves."

He put his arm around her, and Abbey had to remind herself to breathe. She could feel the strength of Gabe's broad shoulders and wanted above all to put her arm around him. Instead, she leaned against the door and flexed her fingers, trying to get some movement back into the frozen muscles. The edges of the clipboard were imprinted in her palms and she recognized the feeling that had weakened her knees before. She was in trouble. She had fallen in love with Gabe Kendall!

LACEY SPRINGER

What an adventure God has given us! Each part of life forms like the petals of a rose around the deep core of faith. Seventeen years of marriage, working as a writer and raising four children has taught me that although things ⬚⬚⬚⬚⬚⬚⬚⬚⬚⬚⬚⬚⬚⬚⬚ life with the Lord is ⬚⬚⬚⬚⬚⬚⬚⬚⬚⬚⬚⬚⬚⬚

D1213461

Dear Reader:

In times like these more and more people are turning to their faith. And they want to read about people like themselves, people who hold the same beliefs dear. If this sounds familiar, you might find that SILHOUETTE INSPIRATIONS are about people like you.

SILHOUETTE INSPIRATIONS are love stories with a difference—they are novels of hope and faith about people who have made a commitment or recommitment of their lives to Christ. And SILHOUETTE INSPIRATIONS are also wonderful romances about men and women experiencing all the joy of falling in love—romances that will touch your heart.

SILHOUETTE INSPIRATIONS—more than just a love story, a love story you'll cherish!

The Editors
SILHOUETTE INSPIRATIONS

WINTER ROSE
Lacey Springer

Silhouette Inspirations

Published by Silhouette Books New York

America's Publisher of Contemporary Romance

Inspirations by Lacey Springer

A Wealth of Love #7
Winter Rose #25

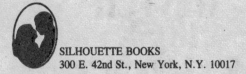

SILHOUETTE BOOKS
300 E. 42nd St., New York, N.Y. 10017

Copyright © 1985 by Lacey Springer
Cover artwork copyright © 1985 Rudy Nappi

Distributed by Pocket Books

ISBN: 0-373-04500-X

First Silhouette Books printing January, 1985

10 9 8 7 6 5 4 3 2 1

America's Publisher of Contemporary Romance

Printed in the U.S.A.

To Roz
"I can no other answer make but thanks, thanks,
and ever thanks."

—William Shakespeare

Chapter One

Abbey took one look in the mirror and grabbed a tissue to blot the excess red from her cheekbones. After all, she wasn't trying out for a play. She took another look, wishing she had a decent mirror instead of the cloudy glass in the old walnut stand.

The brown suit gave her five-foot-four frame the illusion of more height. That was good. The white piping on the suit was turning a slight yellow from age. That was bad. The leather shoes and bag looked new because she had rarely worn them in the two years she had been back. That was good. They were out of style. That was bad.

She shrugged philosophically and went downstairs. The Reverend Ira Wilson was at his desk as she passed down the hall to the front door. He put down his worn Bible as she stopped at his door.

It was easy to see where Abbey's heart-shaped face and warm brown eyes and hair had come from. It was possible to see how distinguished she would look someday with snow-white hair in a halo around a fine-boned face. But where Ira's eyes were compassionate and full of peace, Abbey's were full of the light of determination. Ira knew the signs well. That part of her she had inherited from Elizabeth, his wife.

"Today is your interview," he said encouragingly.

"Yes." Abbey smiled shakily. "I'm a little panicked. It's been a while."

"Just be yourself," Ira advised with paternal pride. "You'll get the job."

"Oh, Dad." Abbey crossed to him and kissed him. "If everyone were like you, life would be much simpler."

"Are you saying I'm simple?" he inquired testily.

"You're so simple, you are complicated," answered his daughter affectionately. "I'm off to see the wizard. Say a prayer or two for me, please."

"I will," he promised as she whirled away and out the door. He could hear the tapping of her rarely worn heels on the porch.

Abbey had to walk five blocks to get to the old cannery. She also had to cross the paths of many of her father's friends, all of whom had known her since she was born. She greeted them affectionately or respectfully, as the situation demanded. Everyone knew she was on her way to interview for the job with the town's economic genius, Gabe Kendall.

Mrs. Shriers was picking the last roses from the bushes by her fence as Abbey swung by. "Hello, dearie. On your way to talk to the big man, I see. You look mighty pretty."

Abbey took the rose Mrs. Shriers handed her and tucked it into the clasp of her purse. "Thank you, Mrs. Shriers. I'll stop by after the interview. I may need the tea and sympathy."

Abbey loved the old lady, as did everyone in the town of Counsel. Millicent Shriers was the first to help and the last to give up on anyone. Her heart was as big as the giant cookies she had fed to generations of Counsel kids. Her mind was as astute and clear in her eighties as it had been in her teens. She put a delicate, withered hand against Abbey's cheek.

"If he lets you pass by, he's too big a fool to run a factory."

Abbey hugged her adopted grandmother and went on to the newly renovated factory grounds. The old fences had not been replaced, as everyone had envisioned. The town had been positive that the brick and wooden façade would be replaced by chrome and glass.

While Kendall Enterprises had spent the summer completely redoing the inside of the factory and adding buildings in the back, the outside of the factory had been restored to its former glory. Even the stone gargoyles above its beveled glass doors were cleaned. The building was a perfect example of turn-of-the-century architecture. It had gone from being a county seat building, to cannery, to warehouse and finally to cannery again.

When the county seat had moved to Jefferson, Iowa, it had been the death knell for Counsel. With the exception of a few stores selling groceries and farming equipment, and the post office in the drugstore, Counsel was dying. When the cannery had revitalized it during World War II, new families had moved into the town to enjoy its temporary prosperity. But the small factory had forever closed its doors in the late sixties, and Counsel had felt its death grip tighten.

Ira Wilson and his contemporaries had fought valiantly to save the town. With faith, they had tried to entice manufacturers and businessmen to their little town in the northern hills of Iowa. They had started planting orchards of apples that had come to be known as the Iowa Nobles. The orchards could not support the whole town, however, and young families moved away to bigger towns that offered better jobs.

It was the apples that had interested Kendall Industries. Hope had blazed again as the representatives of the conglomerate visited the fathers of the town and discussed taxes, jobs and possibilities. It took two years to close the deal. Abbey knew because she had come back home to care for her dying mother. Elizabeth Wilson died on the day after the papers had been signed by the city council and Gabe Kendall.

Abbey had been one of the many young people who had left Counsel to work. At eighteen she had attended business school in Des Moines. She had joined the secretarial pool of a large legal firm in Chicago. She kept working and going to night classes at the University of Chicago, taking legal secretarial courses. She had become an assistant and then executive secretary to a junior partner of the firm, the position she held when the letter came from her father.

Abbey had been Elizabeth and Ira's only and long-awaited child. There was no one else. Fully aware that her job would not be held for her, Abbey packed and went home. She had slipped easily into the old pattern of childhood; only now she was not a child. At first she missed the excitement of her former world. She had spent six years establishing herself, and that was wiped away in the last two years.

She'd known most of the men in her age group since childhood, and she couldn't see them as anything other than old pals with whom she had climbed trees and played games. Everyone expected her to marry Jordan Davis if she stayed in Counsel. He was the only eligible male left in town. He had asked her. She had put him off.

Abbey had put off all decisions for the last six months following her mother's passing. She couldn't help but notice the new fragility of her father since Elizabeth's death. He firmly believed that his dear wife was waiting for him in heaven. He was trying very hard not to selfishly miss her so much. He threw himself into his church affairs, forgetting to eat or rest, letting the Lord's work devour his time until he could accommodate his grief. Abbey feared that if she left, he could see Elizabeth very soon indeed. He was incapable of thinking of himself and was the kind of man who would starve to death while carrying a basket of food to the poor.

Elizabeth had augmented her husband's small income with wonderful gardens. She had been an expert in canning and preserving. Abbey had to manage a way of preserving her father in another way. She needed to use her own talents. Ira would never accept money from his daughter, but she knew he wouldn't notice where the food came from or that the electricity bills were paid.

The problem had been to find a workplace and still keep her eye on Ira. It was a two-hour drive to Des Moines, which meant that she would be driving for four hours a day. The northern Iowa blizzards could maroon her in the big city for days. Then the prayed-for solution had come to Counsel.

The new cannery would be open year round. In the fall they would can the fine Iowa apples. In the winter they would put out home-style beans, chili and hearty soups. In the summer they would utilize the sweet corn that made the state famous.

Vacant houses were already occupied by new families who would work at the cannery. The stores were expanding their stock. A new restaurant had opened. Ira had welcomed the new church members with joy. The rectory and frame church with its hundred-year-old bell tower had received a fresh coat of white paint in celebration.

Abbey entered the foyer of the building, delighted to see that it had been decorated with old prints of Counsel. There was the original Counsel Church, with Abbey's great-grandfather standing outside the front door looking stern and forbidding. She smiled, thinking how much Ira would enjoy that touch. At the end of the room sat a pretty young girl whom Abbey recognized as being new in town.

The young receptionist directed her to the oak-carved staircase. At the top of the stairs another pretty girl directed her down a hallway full of open doors. She waved at many of the people she knew in the offices.

Abbey paused at the door at the end of the hall and drew a deep breath. When Jordan Davis had informed her about an opening for an executive assistant, she had been wary. . . .

"I'm an executive secretary," she'd said. "Why couldn't Mr. Kendall need a secretary?"

Jordan's hazel eyes had looked apologetic. "He brought his own from Chicago. Give it a try, Abbey. The other jobs were filled when you were busy with your mother. This is the only opening that might work for you. The pay is good. Mr. Kendall uses his other executive assistant to travel for him. He wants one assistant from the town for coordination purposes. Who knows this town better than you? After all, your family founded it.''

"You didn't tell him that!'' Abbey had shuddered. "He'll believe the town is trying to pressure him into hiring me.''

"So what?'' had said Jordan realistically. "The town owes your father a lot.''

"I'd rather be hired because I was qualified for the position,'' Abbey had sighed.

"You don't have to work.'' Jordan's eyes had lit up. "Marry me. I can certainly support you and help your father. The farm is in good shape.''

Abbey shook her head to clear away the sad look in Jordan's eyes when she'd refused him again. She squared her shoulders and opened the door in front of her. If she did not get a position at the cannery, she'd have to seriously consider alternatives.

A small woman behind a giant mahogany desk looked up from her typewriter. When Abbey explained who she was, the woman rose and came to shake hands with her.

"You're Pastor Wilson's daughter. I met him many times at the town meetings; he's a charming man. I understand you've both suffered a loss. Please accept my condolences. Mr. Kendall is interviewing another applicant at this moment. May I get you a cup of coffee?''

Well done, thought Abbey. She has just told me in the nicest way possible that they are aware of who I am, and it won't make any difference if I'm not good for the job. Well, good! That's fair.

Just as she sat down in one of the big brown leather chairs and picked up a magazine, the inner office door opened. Abbey's heart sank. The applicant before her was Amy Eisen.

The secretary whisked into the office and closed the door behind her. Amy looked resplendent in a pale mauve suit that complimented her silvery hair and ivory complexion. Touches of gray in the scarf at her neck and her accessories enhanced her gray-green eyes.

"Amy!" Abbey greeted her friend. "You always make me feel like a plain chocolate bar in competition with a French bonbon. You look smashing!"

Amy hugged her old friend. "Quick, before the protecting dragon returns. Let me assure you that I'm not what he wanted. The fact that I've never held a job before was definitely not in my favor."

"Do you really want to work?" Abbey queried. The town banker's daughter had never labored at anything other than dinner parties and shopping as far as Abbey knew.

"I thought it might be interesting," Amy gurgled in her silvery voice. "That was before I met Gabe Kendall. Now I know it would just be hard work. Obviously being decorative is not what he had in mind. He'd be smart to get you. What is there about this town that you don't know?"

The secretary had opened the door and caught the end of the conversation. Lesley Strickler was a fifty-year-old widow. An efficient and talented secretary, she was also a fair and kind woman. She devoutly hoped that the job would not go to the willowy blonde with the tinkling laugh.

"Miss Wilson? Mr. Kendall will see you now."

Abbey smiled at Amy, who winked back and nodded

politely to Lesley. Then she entered the office and closed the door behind her.

Abbey stood quietly by the door, looking at the man who had become the angel for her town. By opening the cannery he had put the town back into production. He had saved the community and brought back prosperity. The children had a future in Counsel once again.

Gabe Kendall did not look like an angel. His hair was the blue-black of his Welsh ancestors. His skin was fair. His physique was more suited to a coal miner than a business-man; when he stood, his wide shoulders filled the window behind him. Abbey blinked. A weird trick of the light made him a black silhouette with the outside sunlight shining around him like a golden mantle. Abbey shivered, though the image disappeared when he came around his desk to shake her hand. His firm mouth smiled politely, but his gray-blue eyes remained expressionless. Abbey felt that nothing could melt those eyes. It was as though the person living behind them were encased in ice.

His voice was deep, but without the friendly warmth that Abbey was used to hearing. She felt as though this impressive man were not there. He said the right things, but they were meaningless because there was no inflection in the words.

He held her resumé in his hands. Abbey corraled her imagination and listened to his question. He'd asked her if she enjoyed working with groups of people.

"I must," she answered honestly. "If I didn't like working in groups, I would have gone mad by the time I was twelve. A preacher's daughter learns to move in a group all of her life." She regretted her humor almost immediately and tried to redeem herself. "I mean I was taught to function in social situations from an early age. The law firm I worked for in Chicago specialized in civil cases. I've had most of my working experience with groups—both large and small."

She could feel the blush work itself up to her cheeks. His silence gave her an irresistible urge to babble on, but she controlled the impulse and sat still with her hands quietly resting in her lap. If the man would show a modicum of friendliness, it would have been one hundred percent easier. She felt incredibly gauche.

Her eyes fell to the long, sensitive hands holding her resumé. He must think she was a total fool. She wasn't. She'd been good at her job; she had been up for another promotion just before her mother's illness. She hadn't realized until now how her confidence had ebbed in two years. Her head lifted again to meet his new question.

"You would be working with groups in the factory, the farms and the orchards. This job would be to coordinate the local elements. I have another assistant who does the interstate coordination for me. Do you think the local people would balk because you are a woman?"

"No," Abbey stated truthfully. "I know the people in this area very well. They won't care what sex I am as long as I deal fairly and honestly with them."

"The hours could be long. It is not necessarily a nine-to-five job," Gabe said flatly.

Abbey thought of the hours of travel to and from Des Moines and tried not to seem too desperate. "I understand that."

"You have excellent references, and I understand why a

two-year absence from the work force was necessary, because of your mother's illness. Are you sure you don't wish to return to the firm you were with? They seem to want you back.''

''Yes, they've been very kind. My problem is that I want to stay with my father. I am all he has. Please don't misunderstand about my father. He's a very independent man with a firm grasp on his faith, his life and his work. He encouraged me to return to my job in Chicago. I simply feel I'd rather stay in Counsel to be near him.''

''I am somewhat familiar with those circumstances,'' Gabe muttered, to Abbey's surprise. ''You have the best qualifications of any of the applicants. You are certainly presentable enough to represent the company. Your recommendations are glowing on both a local and business level. If you have no objections, I would like you to start as soon as possible, since Ross Ellis, my other assistant, is inundated with local problems that are totally unfamiliar to him. For instance, why must the apples from the Davis Orchards be moved in baskets rather than the boxes provided by the company?''

Abbey smiled gratefully. That was easy. ''The baskets are made by the Bailey family for the Davis Orchards. The two families are related by marriage. To box the apples would be to cut the income of a family member. The Baileys would feel betrayed by the Davises.''

Gabe nodded. ''What would you do?''

''Do you have a contract with the people who make the boxes?'' Abbey asked.

''Only for each shipment.''

''I know the Bailey family,'' Abbey ventured. ''They've

done the woodworking and carpentry around this town for over sixty years. If we would contract the boxes to them, it would serve three purposes. We would have a local source instead of an out-of-state source. It would be very good public relations to subcontract to a local, as far as the town is concerned. It would also save transportation fees for the boxes.''

"Good," Gabe reflected. "Yes, I like all three advantages. You can see to it tomorrow. That will be your first assignment. Here's a list of the distributors, the subcontractors and the farmers we deal with here. Mrs. Strickler will show you to your office and introduce you to Ross." He stood politely to dismiss her after ringing for Lesley Strickler.

Outside his door, Abbey took a deep breath and clutched her list.

"Congratulations," offered the secretary. "I'm Lesley Strickler. I take it you have the job."

"Yes," said Abbey faintly. "It all happened rather fast."

"That's the boss," stated Lesley crisply. "I'll show you your office."

Lesley led Abbey to a small office adorned in the same golden oak as the other rooms. She was looking in delight at an old oak news desk when a pleasant tenor interrupted her thoughts of plants and curtains.

"Hi. I hear you're the new left hand."

The figure in her doorway was a lean whippet of a man. His face was long and narrow under light brown hair the same color as his eyes. "I'm Ross Ellis, the right hand. You must be Abbey Wilson, the boss's left hand."

"Oh! Right." Abbey smiled.

"Ah, I can see why the boss hired you, with a smile like that," Ross teased. "Can you work, too?"

"I plan on it," Abbey answered brusquely.

"I wasn't insulting you," Ross insisted. "I've never worked with a lady assistant before. I was trying for charm. I think I got irritation."

Abbey took pity on him. "Your intent is accepted. Your charm is admired, but I really need your expertise more, since I'm not sure what I'm going to be doing."

Lesley appeared at the door with coffee on a tray. "Don't let him throw you off, Abbey. He's very good at his job. He just pretends to act like a fool so that the ladies will feel sorry for him."

Ross took a cup of coffee and perched on the corner of Abbey's desk. "It's hard when Lesley gives my act away. She's always on the side of the female. It's tough for a poor male to make his way with Lesley protecting all of the pretty girls in the office."

"Hmmmmmph!" snorted Lesley. "Now, you get down to business and tell Abbey what she needs to know."

The rest of the afternoon was spent learning about the duties of her new job. Lesley had been right. Ross was a fund of information and good sense when he got down to business. The rather silly dilettante who came into her office originally had little to do with the sharp, intelligent instructor who stayed to help. Five more lists were added to her collections before she left the office. By then she had a good idea of what was expected of her, thanks to Ross and Lesley.

At five o'clock Abbey was descending the stairs between her two mentors, thanking them fervently, when a cool voice from above interrupted her.

"I'm glad to see that my team is already in action, but I hadn't intended for Miss Wilson to start working the day I hired her."

Abbey looked up at the tall man on the landing above. "I wanted to begin learning today," she blurted. "I'm grateful to Mr. Ellis and Mrs. Strickler for giving me so much of their valuable time."

The frozen eyes regarded her. "Yes. Well. We will see you tomorrow, Miss Wilson." He seemed to vanish into the dark hall behind him.

Abbey, Lesley and Ross stood on the stairs like three children who had been chastised by a teacher for something they hadn't done.

Abbey was still staring open-mouthed at the empty space just occupied by her new boss when Ross's soft voice broke into her thoughts.

"In the old days he would have joined us and treated us all to dinner on your first day, Abbey."

Lesley made a tch-tching sound. "He has changed so much since it happened."

They continued down the stairs in a somber mood. Ross opened the door for the ladies. "It's been a nightmare for him. I'm beginning to wonder if he'll ever get over it."

Abbey felt at a distinct disadvantage. She knew that her two companions took it for granted that she knew what incident they were referring to. She hesitated to state her ignorance baldly for fear it was something that was none of her business. Bewildered, she kept silent.

"I think starting the factory from scratch like this is very good for him," Lesley commented.

"Maybe," Ross conceded. "Frankly, I think it gives him too much time to think about things. There was always something to do in the city to take your mind off your problems. Counsel folds its wings and buries itself from dusk to dawn. I've read more books in the last two months than I have in the last two years.''

"I love it,'' Lesley said with a soft emphasis. "I was a small-town girl to begin with, so I'm happy to return. In the spring I'll have a little garden of my own. I'm going to plant a million pansies around my porch. On my vacation next year, I'm going to sit on my porch swing and watch the town go by and wave at people.''

"I found myself more lonely in Chicago than in Counsel,'' volunteered Abbey. "It's easy to get lost in a crowd, and it seems so much worse to be alone when you're surrounded by people.''

"I don't see why Gabe didn't just retire and go on a trip around the world. When he and his father liquidated the conglomerate, they accrued more money than ten men could spend in a lifetime. Why start all over again at the bottom?'' Ross shook his head disgustedly. "I don't mean to bite the hand that feeds me. It does seem odd to bury yourself in the Iowa hills and manufacture applesauce.''

"Some men need to work,'' stated Lesley wisely. "He isn't the kind of man who could be happy doing nothing. He's accomplishing a great deal here, and it takes all of his waking time to solve the problems of a new beginning.''

"The town is grateful beyond telling,'' Abbey reminded them. "It's also a new beginning for Counsel. The cannery saved the town.''

Lesley's clear gray eyes warmed toward Abbey. "I think that's what he was after, Abbey. By saving the town, he's hoping to find a way to save himself.''

They had reached Lesley's little bungalow with its tiny

square of green outlined by a white picket fence. Lesley invited Abbey and Ross in for a snack, but Abbey was eager to share the news of her good fortune with her father. Ross accepted Lesley's offer and together they waved Abbey down the street.

Abbey walked thoughtfully toward the business center of Counsel, wondering exactly what Gabe Kendall needed to forget.

Chapter Two

To celebrate her new job, Abbey stopped off at the grocery store and bought two thick steaks for supper. Jo Ellen Payne, wife of the owner, took one look at the steaks and enveloped her in a huge hug. "You got the job!"

Fred came around the meat counter to shake her hand. "We knew you'd get it. Hiring a Wilson is one of the smartest things Mr. Kendall could do."

By the time Abbey had escaped the good wishes of the Payne family, it was nearing six o'clock and dusk had swept everyone to the dinner table.

Ira was opening a can of beans when Abbey entered the kitchen with her treasure. Neb, the dog Ira had found half-drowned in a nearby creek, was eating something in a corner. His St. Bernard tail on a shepherd body whisked a hello to Abbey while his jaws continued crunching. Ira had named him Nebuchadnezzar after the King of Babylon because Neb was such an honest pagan who wouldn't stop chasing the neighborhood cats. He wouldn't stop until Sheba came to live with them after having been abandoned on the highway by some vacationing family. Sheba had civilized Neb quickly by shredding his nose on a series of battlefields. Now the large gray female cat sat on a kitchen chair cleaning her paws. Neb never ate until Sheba was finished. He valued his large black nose intact.

"Dad!" sang Abbey. "Don't open those beans. We have steaks for dinner!"

Ira's eyes twinkled. "That means you got the job."

They talked while she popped the steaks into the broiler of the large old stove and put together a salad. Ira smiled when told of the meeting with Amy in the outer office.

Abbey placed the thick, sizzling steaks on the table. "Millicent Shriers sent some of her cookies for dessert. I'd promised to let her know if I got the job."

Ira's eyes sparkled. "Actually, about three people from the cannery called to tell me you had the job, but I didn't want to spoil your fun."

Quickly he bowed his head to say grace, effectively cutting off any comments Abbey might have made. She smiled to herself. Sometimes it could be really annoying to have everyone know your business. Usually it was like having an extended family who cared and rejoiced for you.

It was while they were enjoying Millicent's fruit cookies that Abbey got to Gabe Kendall. "He seems so hard. He has the most forbidding manner, Dad. Talk about an intimidating presence! He scared me silly."

"He sounds a lot like his father," Ira mused. "Ralph was a big, imposing man when we were young. Some people misunderstood him. They thought he was hostile when he was really shy.''

''Dad! When did you know Ralph Kendall?''

''We were in the seminary together,'' Ira explained. ''I always thought Ralph left the seminary and went into the family business because of his effect on people. He was a prince of a man. He was absolutely honest, but not very diplomatic. He had a cutting way of telling the truth that put people off.''

''Tell me about the family. Why is the son so frozen?''

''I only knew the boys when they were babies. Ralph married Meg two months after I married your mother. We were best men at each other's weddings. They had the boys right away. You were born much later.

''We used to write,'' Ira continued, ''but the last few years before the accident, we'd sort of gotten down to just exchanging Christmas cards. I remember we sent a wedding present when Gabriel got married.''

''His name is Gabriel? He's married?'' Abbey felt disappointed. ''I'm surprised. He didn't seem married.''

Ira's voice took on a reproving tone. ''That's how young women get into trouble, my dear. A great many men don't seem married when they are. Actually, he is a widower.''

Abbey was mesmerized by her father's story. ''Was that the accident you mentioned?''

''The Kendalls have a beautiful summer place on Mackinac Island. The whole family was supposed to fly there for a vacation. The younger boy, Michael, was a pilot. Let's see. Gabe and his wife, Ann, had twins about two years old, Raphael II, named for his grandfather, and little Rachel.''

''All names from the Bible?''

''All names of angels,'' Ira corrected. ''Raphael, Gabriel

and Michael. Those names had been passed down the male line in Ralph's family for years.''

"Go on, Dad,'' Abbey urged.

"Well, that was it. They didn't make it to the island. A sudden storm came up and caught them. The plane crashed into Lake Huron.''

"But Gabe and his father survived.''

"Some kind of business deal had come up. Ralph and Gabe were going to join the others later. That's why they weren't on the plane.''

"When did this happen?'' Abbey refilled her father's milk glass as he reached for another cookie.

"About two years ago. I know it was before I called Ralph about opening a factory here. I was calling any of my old friends who could help about then. That's when I found out about the accident, because Ralph was just recovering from his heart attack.''

"Oh no!'' protested Abbey.

"If Gabe is anything like his father, I would imagine that his apparent coldness masks his real feelings. The harder he seems on the outside, the more pain he has on the inside.'' Ira's eyes darkened in sympathy. "It's always more difficult for men like that. Suffering is something they find embarrassing, so they try to bury it deep within themselves. It tends to make them savage, like a dog biting his own paw because he won't let someone remove the thorn.''

"I think in this case, Dad, the thorn is out but the wound won't heal. To lose your mother, wife, children and brother at the same time would leave a terrible hole in your heart,'' Abbey said gravely.

They were both silent for a moment, reminded of the loved one missing from their own table. Their own grief made them mute. They could well understand the need of a heart filled with loss.

Later that night, Abbey sat on the old window seat with Sheba purring in her lap and stared at the harvest moon rising high and red in the sky. How many romantic fantasies she had woven in her girlhood around that particular moon! It was the time of new crushes in high school, giggling walks in the park and a terrible vulnerability to the whole world.

She had hardly noticed it in the city, but in the countryside its magical domination was impossible to ignore. She opened her window to the crisp September night and breathed deeply of the autumn-tinged air. She was no longer a child, but she still found living a great adventure. Tomorrow was a new beginning.

The moon held no lure for the still figure of the tall man sitting alone on the top floor of the factory. Often he hardly differentiated between the nights and days. The work light over his desk was his moon, and the papers in front of him were his life.

The next day Abbey came early to work with a notebook and a large philodendron in tow. The plant went on the corner of her desk while the notebook resided in the middle, ready for action.

She called the Davis farm and made arrangements to visit Zeb and Emma within the hour. She knew that the phone could not replace face-to-face contact with people like the Davises.

Driving up the winding road to the farm, she noticed the apples hanging heavily on the thick trees. They would be ready for picking within the next few weeks.

"They look wonderful this year," she exclaimed to Zeb Davis as he greeted her at the car. "I'm so glad the first year at the cannery is a particularly good year for the Nobles."

Zeb's long, lined face broke into a pleased grin. "Yep, they've outdone themselves this season. Jordan said you got the job at the cannery. Mother's inside with cinnamon rolls and cider. You better come on in. Jordan won't be good for anything else till you've left."

Abbey followed Zeb into the enormous country kitchen ruled by his plump, practical wife, Emma. Emma Davis was one of the hardest-working ladies in the county and one of the most formidable. She was president of the women's circle at the church and of the farmers' wives' organization in town. Though she was good-hearted and kind, nobody put one over on Emma Davis.

It took a short time to work out the box problem at the immense oak table.

"Sounds good," pronounced Zeb. "We'll use the baskets to pick because that's what our workers are used to, but we'll pack 'em on the trucks in the boxes. That way we can use the baskets we've got while Charlie Bailey makes the cannery boxes. Turns out fine for everybody."

"It was a real smart thing for Gabe Kendall to hire you," announced Emma. "That other fellow was friendly enough, but he was kinda pushy. Zeb was getting real annoyed with him."

Jordan threw his advice into the pot. "He's strictly a city boy, the kind that dresses like a magazine ad. He's probably great in town, but not so hot out here." Jordan's voice took on a worried note. "You don't have to work with him a lot, do you, Abbey?"

Abbey smiled to herself. She knew where Jordan was

coming from. She was saved an answer by the barking dogs outside announcing another visitor.

Zeb looked out the window. "It's your boss, Abbey. Is he checking up on you already?"

"I hope not." Abbey looked out at the big man unfolding himself from the station wagon. "It's only my first day."

She was sitting at the table when Gabe entered the kitchen with Zeb, who was making stoutly reassuring statements about Abbey's abilities.

"She solved the problem in a few minutes that took your city fella a week to work on. It was a real smart thing to hire a Wilson. Heck, they've been solving problems in Counsel for three generations."

Abbey felt herself blush. Zeb was laying it on a bit thick.

Gabe's face nearly flickered into a smile. "I can see that. No, I'm just here to see the Nobles. They're looking good. We'll be ready to go in two weeks. The weather has favored our interests this year."

"The Lord has truly blessed us," corrected Emma, primly setting a plate of rolls on the table. "Sit down and rest your feet, Mr. Kendall."

Gabe sat down facing Abbey and took a roll.

"I hear you've taken over the old Johnson place," Jordan said. "You going to make that into more orchards?"

"No," Gabe said stiffly. "I'm going to live there with my father. He's always wanted a farm to retire on. We'll do some planting. There's already some Jonathans to the east of the house."

"Maybe your dad would like to join the men's club," suggested Zeb. "We do a lot of different things. There are several retired fellas in the club."

Gabe's tone seemed to freeze out the Davises. "He's in a

wheelchair recovering from a major heart attack. I doubt if he'd be too interested in that kind of thing.''

The table fell silent. Abbey tried to rescue the conversation.

''I used to play with the Johnson kids when we were little. I loved that big old house. I remember we used to roller-skate three abreast in the second-floor hall. You could see the whole countryside from the second-floor windows. It's a lovely house.''

''Those wide halls are good for a wheelchair,'' Gabe commented dryly.

''When is your father coming?'' asked Emma.

''This weekend. The furniture is supposed to be delivered today. I have my other assistant waiting patiently at the house. I'd like to take a look at your cider room, Mr. Davis, if it's all right with you. One of the men at the cannery said you had invented something called red cider?''

''Oh,'' said Emma delightedly, ''you mean my red cinnamon cider. We'll be glad to show you. It's from my grandmother's recipe.''

''I'll be getting back to the office,'' said Abbey, excusing herself. ''I'll stop off at the Bailey farm on my way and get Charlie's price list for Mr. Kendall.''

Jordan walked her to her car while Gabe Kendall went on to the cider room in the barn with the elder Davises. Jordan was shaking his head. ''He isn't one for friendly conversation, is he?''

Abbey had to agree, but she felt honor-bound to explain the background to Jordan lest the Davises decide against Mr. Kendall. Jordan's sympathy was quickly won by the story.

''No wonder he's not friendly. I'll tell the folks so they

won't think it's them. Mom will take him right to heart and marry him off. You'll see. He'll feel better when he gets a good wife and starts a new family. Life has to go on.''

Abbey drove away with Jordan's words in her ears. "Life has to go on." She knew that the old platitude was basically true, but she wondered how easily Jordan would have said that if it had been his family who was lost.

She loved the Davises. Jordan was like a big brother. Everything was so simple for him. You had your rules and you obeyed them. If you obeyed, life went well; if you disobeyed, you were punished. The trouble was that sometimes you got punished when there had been no crime. Jordan had never come across that situation, but Gabe Kendall certainly had. Jordan had never wanted to leave the area he was born in. Gabe had left the city he knew for a countryside he was unfamiliar with. Jordan's parents were both alive and healthy. Gabe had lost one parent and had to care for the other. Her father had an old piece of advice that fit this situation. "Don't judge another until you have walked in his shoes." Guiltily Abbey admitted to herself that sometimes Jordan bored her to tears. If she loved him, she wouldn't be comparing him to another man.

One hour and two ciders later, Abbey appeared at the office with a price list in hand. A typewriter, a bookcase and a supply of paper had been placed in her office. Lesley had left her several phone numbers to call, along with a company production timetable. Two calls concerned deadlines. Referring to the timetable, she informed the farmers when they should expect to begin delivering apples. Ross called to request that she make some of his calls to the trucking agencies, since he was still waiting for the boss's furniture.

"It'd better arrive this afternoon." Ross was obviously irritated. "I'm supposed to catch a plane to Chicago this evening. I've got to leave here by four o'clock to reach the airport on time."

Abbey assured him she would take care of the calls. She finished making Ross's calls and her own to keep the farmers informed of the production schedule. She had just completed the last one when the phone rang at 4:30 P.M. It was Ross.

"Abbey, you've got to get out here. As it is, I'm running it close. I won't even be able to get back to my motel and get my clothes. I'm leaving right now. The key is under the flowerpot on the front right window. See you next week!"

When she arrived at the Johnson place, she found a note with the key: "The list of furniture placements is on the kitchen counter. I left some coffee on for you. Ross."

She stood in the middle of the grand old farmhouse and seemed to hear the echo of childhood laughter all around her. She had been to many teenage gatherings in this house, as the Johnson's four children were all girls. Abbey stood in the immense bay window that looked out on the rolling fields, which had been rented to a neighboring farmer.

All four girls had married and moved away. The Johnsons had retired and moved to the city to be near their children and grandchildren. Now the house would belong to two men who lived in grief. That was a shame. This house cried out for a large, happy family full of life and vitality.

The arrival of two big vans interrupted her thoughts.

The moving men were still unloading the Kendalls' beautiful possessions at 7 P.M. when Abbey called her father to tell him not to wait supper for her. "They've only unloaded one of the vans, Dad. I've never seen so much furniture. It's really old. Some of the tables look like they belong in a museum. It's overwhelming!''

"Well, don't let it overwhelm you too much," quipped Ira. "We can't afford to redecorate the rectory without the Kendall money to go with it.''

"I'm the one who's realistic," Abbey retorted, laughing. "I've got to run because I've got the list of where things go. See you later.''

The list merely gave the room the furniture went in, so Abbey had to make some fast decisions about the placement of the furniture.

First the ornamental rugs were laid on the wall-to-wall carpeting. There was no carpeting in the kitchen. Abbey loved that room with its country fireplace and brass fixtures. She couldn't resist running her hand over the satin finish of the oak trestle table. The patina of the wood testified to its having been passed down for many years in the Kendall family.

All of the heavy furniture was in position by 8:30 P.M., but the drivers had left boxes of dishes, linens and books that still needed to be unpacked. She felt that Gabe could shelve his own books in the library, but it would be hard for men to put away dishes and pots and pans. She proceeded to attack the kitchen.

She unpacked a box of dishes so fragile that they were transparent and knew they must be meant for the big walnut cabinet in the dining room. Carefully she took a small stack of the delicate china plates from the box and started to carry them into the next room. She turned to face Gabe Kendall. His eyes were so full of agony that she stopped dead in her tracks.

"Please, put those down," he rasped.

Abbey almost dropped the plates in her eagerness to be rid of them. The thick wool carpets had muffled his approach. He had simply appeared in a house that she'd thought was empty. She gently set the plates on the kitchen table.

"You were not hired to do this," Gabe reproved tightly.

"Ross had to leave for Chicago," Abbey hastened to explain. "I thought I'd put these things away in case you wanted to use the kitchen."

"It's not necessary," Gabe said acidly. "I've hired some women to come in tomorrow morning to do that. Those dishes are not to be unpacked at all. You seem to take a great deal upon yourself, Miss Wilson. I prefer people to function in the jobs they are hired to do."

Abbey felt like a nosy busybody who had been poking about in someone else's private business. She untied the dish towel from around her waist and turned away from him to blink back the tears of mortification that had sprung to her eyes. Years of training held. When she turned back to him, she was her usual disciplined self. Without a word she passed him in the doorway and went to get her sweater and purse in the dining room.

"I apologize, Mr. Kendall. Good night."

Gabe heard the hall door open and close. He stood in the doorway until he heard the car pull away. He knew he had overreacted, but he couldn't share with Abbey the reason why he had. He barely knew this woman. He had only really known one other woman.

He had walked into the new house with its old, familiar furniture arranged just as he had envisioned it. It was placed the way he and Ann would have placed it. He had heard a woman humming to herself in the kitchen. Two years had been momentarily wiped out when he had reached the doorway only to find dark-haired Abbey with Ann's dishes in her hands. His brief hope had plummeted to his feet. There was dark-haired Abbey instead of his light-haired wife. Brown eyes instead of blue looked into his. For a second he hated Abbey because she was not his beloved Ann. He knew that he was being unreasonable, that Abbey was innocent of any wrongdoing. It was simply that the pain flowing through him had needed a target, and Abbey had been there.

He picked up a porcelain plate covered with tiny blue flowers. It was unjust that a beautiful object should survive when a beautiful soul had not. Carefully he packed each dish back in the box and closed the lid with the finality of an inner decision.

The next day was Saturday. Abbey was relieved that she would not have to face Gabe Kendall until Monday. It wasn't until later that night that she understood Gabe's reaction.

Emma Davis had brought over chrysanthemums for the sanctuary. They had just finished decorating the pulpit for the next day's services when it hit Abbey. Emma had mentioned that one of her friends had helped set the Kendall house "to rights."

"Mabel said they were sure impressed with the furniture and all. She told Mr. Kendall that some of his things were nicer than the antiques in our museum. He asked her if the museum would like a set of antique dishes for their collection. They were over a hundred years old and had belonged to his wife, he said. They were too valuable to just lie around, and he figured she would enjoy knowing they were somewhere being enjoyed by others. Mabel said they were just beautiful, all covered with blue forget-me-nots. She was real excited.''

Emma bustled off to start preparations for Sunday lunch while Abbey turned off the church lights. Now she understood Gabe's peculiar reaction to her last night.

How terrible it must have been for him to walk into his house and find a stranger handling his wife's things! She sat on the sanctuary steps in deep thought. Why hadn't she just minded her own business and done the job she had been asked to do? She should have realized that he would have made arrangements for things to be put away. However, she had always been trained to put her hand to whatever needed doing. In Counsel you didn't stop doing a job until it was finished. Of course, Gabe Kendall would be unfamiliar with barn raisings, harvest parties, country weddings and christenings where everyone just pitched in.

She leaned her head against the hundred-year-old pulpit with its satin finish. The smell of Emma's flowers permeated the air, and the quiet peace of the church surrounded her. Though she should have felt sorry for this man who had suffered such a loss, she found herself feeling sorry for herself because she had never known that kind of love to lose.

Abbey was a person in two worlds. She loved Counsel and the people in it. She had grown up believing in love and marriage. It wasn't until she had gone away to work that a career had become so important. There were men who were interested in her, but she was not interested in them. They had wanted a smart, sophisticated wife who would give lovely dinner parties and raise intelligent children in the suburbs. The Counsel men wanted a traditional woman who would raise children in the old ways of their fathers. No one ever seemed to see Abbey as the person she was. She loved the traditional ways, but she wanted a more modern role in a man's life. She wanted a man she could talk to about more than his work, his business and his problems. She wanted to share a life. Abbey hungered for the unique partnership her own parents had shared. The man had not yet come along who could draw her in that way. Now, at twenty-six, she was beginning to question her decisions. Should she compromise and marry someone like Jordan? Would she come to love him through the years as some of her old girl friends said she would? Should she have chosen one of those rising young executives?

She raised her eyes to the stained-glass window above the choir loft. No, she had never learned to compromise with the truth, and she would not start now. She had to love before marriage or she would not marry. There were worse things than being an old maid. She smiled to herself at the phrase "old maid." In Chicago she was considered a bachelor girl.

Gabe Kendall had suffered pangs of remorse all night. His rigid sense of fairness had troubled him often in the last few hours. His sense of chivalry was outraged; he had badly treated a woman who was only trying to help him. Finally he had succumbed to his conscience and driven to the rectory. Ira had directed him to the church.

He found Abbey sitting like a child with her arms wrapped around her knees, gazing up at the stained-glass window. The light shone on her upturned face with its liquid brown eyes and sweetly curved lips. He was feeling worse and worse. Only a monster would have picked on this particular woman. He cleared his throat to gain her attention.

Abbey was startled. She recognized him immediately, even in the shadows. "You have a habit, Mr. Kendall, of appearing from nowhere." She chuckled.

"Perhaps, Miss Wilson," Gabe said with dry humor, "it's because you have a habit of daydreaming, so that it seems that way."

Glory, thought Abbey to herself. He's come to fire me! He's too much of a gentleman to do it by phone. Why didn't I keep my mouth shut?

Gabe stalked over to sit beside her, looking out into the pews. "As a matter of fact, I've come to apologize to you for my rudeness last night."

Abbey let out a thankful sigh. "I didn't mean to take liberties."

"I know," said Gabe distantly. "I was the one who jumped to a stupid conclusion. Please accept my humble apologies."

Abbey couldn't stop herself from smiling at his use of the word "humble." It would be hard to imagine this arrogant man sitting next to her as humble. She glanced at the strong profile and noticed that his eyelashes were unusually long and swept the high cheekbones. It gave him an oddly vulnerable quality.

He noticed her scrutiny and became uncomfortable. "I believe I owe you an explanation."

"Not at all," Abbey reassured him. "It was obvious I had unwittingly handled something with a great deal of personal value, and it upset you. I should have been more sensitive. You'll have to forgive me. I'll tell you what—you forgive me, I'll forgive you and we'll forget about the whole thing."

He extended a hand to her. "Done?"

She let him take her hand. "Done."

"I wish all misunderstandings were cleared up as easily," he said wearily.

Abbey considered his statement seriously. "Is it impossible for people to deal with each other truthfully?"

"Not impossible, just improbable," Gabe said wryly.

"With all due respect," Abbey ventured, "I think honesty is the simplest and most practical way of succeeding. Eventually dishonesty is found out by everyone and the business venture is doomed. Whereas, if you have a good reputation, people trust you and your product."

"So speaks the preacher's kid," Gabe taunted.

"You may be a greater sinner from your point of view, Mr. Kendall," acknowledged Abbey, "but I'll bet I know a great deal more about sinners than you do."

Gabe actually smiled, and Abbey nearly fell off the step from shock.

"And you've gained this extensive knowledge from Counsel, Iowa, and a lawyer's office, I take it," he said with a chuckle.

Abbey looked at him levelly. "Even if I'd never left Counsel, I would know a great deal about human nature, Mr. Kendall. Human nature is the same. The sins are thousands of years old. Sinners aren't terribly inventive. Greed today is the same whether the businessman is selling bricks for the pyramids or for a condominium. Even the wicked prefer to deal with an honest man."

"Yes, so they can cheat him," Gabe stated.

"Why would you equate honesty with idiocy?" asked Abbey bluntly. "My father says that your father is a prince. That means he's a good man in all ways. He also believes you're like him. It seems to me that your business has prospered because of your honesty."

Gabe rose and walked away into the shadows again. "The business has prospered, but I have not."

Abbey stood up in the light. She longed to say something comforting to this man, whose pain touched her deeply, more so because he refused to acknowledge it or ask for help.

Impulsively she took a step toward his retreating back. "Mr. Kendall, my father and I know something about grief. Why don't you come to church this Sunday? It might lighten your burden. The Lord can help."

Heavily his dark voice came from the shadows. "You're asking me to get help from the One who has condemned me. Look in Lamentations 3:6."

The door opened and closed behind him. Abbey, dejected, looked through the Bible on the pulpit until she came to Lamentations. What she read chilled her soul.

"He hath set me in dark places, as they that be dead of old."

Chapter Three

The rest of September and October flew by as the cannery swung into full production. Abbey was kept busy with coordinating and communicating her boss's orders. She was never alone with him again, except to receive new directives. Ira had advised her to keep Gabe in her prayers and let the Lord handle the rest. She had resolved to do just that.

Lesley Strickler and Abbey were sharing a lunch table in the company cafeteria when Ross dropped into a vacant chair and sighed pathetically. He waited for a kind female word, which Lesley provided, before he shared his woes with them.

"The boss says I can't take off Thanksgiving. He's worried about the shift to the soups. I told him the distributors are lined up and everything is set. He just fixed me with that steely blue gaze of his and gave me a super-firm refusal. I can have Thanksgiving off, but not the next day. Who wants to spend a holiday eating diner food? I don't think the restaurant is even open on Thanksgiving.''

Abbey grinned. "It's not, but the Wilson restaurant is. You're welcome to spend Thanksgiving with us. Lesley is coming. We'd love to have you, if you don't mind working for your dinner.''

"I was a boy scout." Ross flexed one arm. "I can cut wood for the stove.''

"We've got to get you out of that motel," threatened Abbey. "You seem to think we're still living in colonial times. I have a perfectly good gas stove to cook on, thank you. We also have electricity in the rest of the house, not to mention an indoor bathroom. Honestly, Ross, you need to get out and meet the town.''

"Forget it," said Ross glumly. "You think I don't know that they call me 'that city slicker'? I just don't get on with these people. My jokes fall flat. There are fifteen-minute pauses in the conversation. They don't go for me. I know it's Miss Abbey Wilson they want to deal with, not me!''

"You're exaggerating," remonstrated Abbey. "Give them a chance.''

"They won't give me a chance," insisted Ross. "Besides, you're doing fine. I'm good where I am. I don't need to be popular with the natives.''

Lesley shook a motherly finger at him. "Ross Ellis, you're a snob.''

Ross flashed his charming grin. "Madame Strickler, I am a realist." He stood up and bowed to the two women. "I'm also a survivor. I accept with pleasure Abbey's kind invitation, and I'll be delighted to do any work necessary to earn my meal.'' He started to leave and turned with a twinkle in his toffee eyes. ''Within reason, of course.''

Lesley exchanged a meaningful glance with Abbey. ''I wonder how he'll react when he finds out what the work is.''

''There they are,'' fluted a familiar voice.

Abbey looked up to see Amy Eisen flanked by her father and Gabe Kendall. Lesley raised her eyebrows to Abbey but said nothing as the taller woman glided over to them, her silver furs brushing small tables in her wake.

''I was beginning to think that Gabe kept you chained up in a dungeon somewhere.'' The sapphire on Amy's hand glittered as she carelessly pulled off her gloves. The simplicity of her antique blue suit shouted its price.

Abbey carefully picked her friend's fur out of her dish of chili before it drowned. Amy leaned across the table to whisper in Abbey's ear while Lesley plucked the other end of the offending fur from her beef stew.

''I'm really glad you got the job, Abbey. I would have been absolutely dismal at it. We've been touring the factory.'' Amy leaned back, and one of the assembly-line girls tripped over the trailing fur. While Lesley and Abbey were rescuing the fur, Emil Eisen and Gabe threaded their way to the table.

Emil shook his head at his daughter. ''I told you that thing would be inappropriate for the tour. You've practically strangled every worker we've passed with it.'' The town's banker greeted Abbey like the old friend he was, asking after her father. Gabe had no choice but to join them, as the Eisens were firmly entrenched.

''I'm going to have some of that chili, if Amy's animal is out of the way,'' Emil commented.

Amy rolled the fur in a ball and looked helpless until Abbey cheerfully stowed it away under the cashier's cage for her. Lesley rose and announced that she had to get back to work. Abbey mentioned that her lunch hour was nearly over, but was overruled by the Eisens.

"If I don't get to eat lunch with you, Abbey Wilson, I'll make sure the next payroll is short," Emil threatened comically.

Abbey still hesitated until Gabe signaled her to stay. She thought of Emil as a kindly uncle, and Amy thought of Ira in the same way. The two girls had been like sisters since they were in kindergarten together. Both had been only children, so they had adopted each other.

When Amy's mother had died, Abbey's mother and father had been delighted to have another little girl around. Emil had never worried about his daughter in the hands of the Wilsons.

Abbey knew that Amy was foolish in many ways. She was somewhat spoiled and often careless of other people's feelings, especially male people's. But there was Wilson influence in her personality, too. Amy was never mean or deliberately cruel. Many women in the town did not approve of her and could not understand the friendship between Amy and Abbey. In high school they had been called the "double A's." Only Abbey knew how much her friend had missed a mother. Only Abbey knew how lonely Amy was.

But at the moment Abbey was enjoying the way her friend wove the conversation into areas that made them all laugh. Even Gabe Kendall was smiling. She was relating the story of how she failed typing class in high school in spite of Abbey's best efforts to help her. The teacher had finally thrown her out of class when she had used red fingernail polish to "white out" a typing mistake because she had misplaced her correction fluid.

"You see," she explained, "three fourths of the paper was in red. I think I made forty mistakes out of a possible forty-five words."

"You weren't that bad," demurred Abbey.

"I was probably worse," Amy chirped.

Lunch ended on that note of laughter. Abbey took leave of her friends and marched firmly back to work.

Lesley looked a little dour as she passed the office. "I'm awfully glad you got this job, Abbey. That girl seems like a real nitwit."

Abbey hastened to Amy's defense. "Oh, Lesley, you'd like her if you really got to know her. She wouldn't do well in this kind of job because it's not her kind of thing. Amy knew that the day she interviewed. Her real problem is that she never had to work, so she never developed any skills."

"Oh, I wouldn't say she hadn't developed some skills," commented Lesley.

"Amy would tell you that her chosen vocation was to be decorative." Abbey smiled.

"She does that very well," conceded Lesley dryly. "She's after the boss."

Abbey considered Lesley's statement and agreed that she might be right. "It would be very good for him if Amy did go after him. She's perfect for what he needs. She could fill that old house with people and laughter, and she's a wonderful hostess. It might be just the thing!"

"Good grief, Abbey!" Lesley's voice had a peculiar edge to it. "I think that girl would drive him crazy. He never was a great extrovert, but she'd drive him into becoming a hermit. It's bad enough that he never seems to leave the factory. He's here when I get here and he's here when I leave. I know he must go home occasionally, but I can't figure out when.''

"Doesn't his father's living here make a difference?'' Abbey hadn't heard anything about Ralph Kendall, although the older man had now been in residence for nearly two months. Ira had left numerous messages for his old friend, but they had gone unanswered.

"It doesn't seem to,'' said Lesley glumly. "Of course, old Mr. Kendall was much more straitlaced than Gabe. The heart attack made a complete invalid of him. I know they have a nurse who lives with them because I make out her paychecks every week. There can't be much home life.''

Abbey looked at her troubled friend. "Maybe Amy could help.''

Lesley sighed. "Remember your first day, Abbey? In the old days he would have taken us all out to coffee so we could get acquainted. Now he just appears and disappears with orders to be obeyed. It's rather depressing. I like this town, and I love my little house, but I'm thinking of taking another job back in Chicago. It hurts too much to see him like this.''

"Lesley,'' pleaded Abbey, "wait awhile. At least give him a chance to change. It would be a killer for him to lose his executive secretary now. The changeover to the soup line is coming at the end of the month. Wait until you see Counsel at Christmas and Easter—you'll never want to leave us.''

Lesley gave Abbey a quick hug. "You really are a dear, Abbey. I hope that man has sense enough to appreciate what you've done for him.''

"I've just done my job," Abbey protested. "Don't give me credit I don't deserve."

"Hmmmmm," said Lesley. "I've just had a marvelous idea. Your father was a great friend of Ralph Kendall's, wasn't he?"

"They were in each other's weddings." Abbey wondered what was causing that gleam in Lesley's eyes.

"I'm going to take off early." Lesley headed toward her own office. "Will you answer my phone for me, please? I've got an important errand to do."

Bewildered at Lesley's sudden mood change, Abbey agreed. She had little time to think of her friend's suspicious behavior for the rest of the afternoon, between answering the phones and doing her own work. She was just wrapping up a conversation with the cold-room foreman when Gabe appeared at the door with some papers in his hand.

"Where's Lesley?" he demanded. "These letters have to go out tonight."

"She had to take off early," Abbey explained. "I can type them for you."

"Can you type?" he asked dubiously.

"I was a legal secretary. I can probably manage a letter or two without falling apart, Mr. Kendall."

"Did you talk to your lawyer with that degree of impertinence, Miss Wilson?" Gabe inquired innocently.

"No, sir," Abbey answered him civilly. "He never questioned my competence or my abilities on so basic an issue." Abbey was rather proud of that sentence. It was efficient and honest without inviting a real reprimand.

"You are an interesting dichotomy, Miss Wilson. You seem so sweet and soft, but you have an effective sting in your personality. I didn't mean to offend you. I'm just desperate. These letters really must go out today."

Abbey gently took the letters from him. "If you'll return to your office, Mr. Kendall, I'll bring you the letters when they're ready to sign."

The letters were very easy to do, since she merely had to retype corrected drafts of Lesley's fine typing. Abbey delivered them to Gabe's office in record time, then went back to her own office and prepared to leave for the day. She had slipped on her sweater when she turned to find him at her door once again.

"Is there something wrong?" she asked.

"I wondered if you might consider letting me buy you dinner tonight, since it's after seven."

Abbey was surprised both by the time and by the invitation. She hadn't realized it was that late. Had her father already eaten? Should she offer Gabe the hospitality of her home?

"Let me give my father a ring and see what his plans are," she said, picking up the phone. There was no answer at the house. That meant that Ira had eaten and gone to a meeting, or had accepted a dinner invitation elsewhere.

"Well?" Gabe persisted. "What's the prognosis? Will you join me for dinner or not?"

"Won't your father miss you?" asked Abbey, stalling for time.

"He eats on the dot of five," Gabe said impatiently. "I don't usually have to ask permission of my father, his nurse or the cat to dine out. I feel old enough to manage these decisions on my own. Aren't you able to do the same?"

"Yes, of course," agreed Abbey. "I didn't want you to

feel you were beholden because I typed a few letters. I was just giving you a polite way of getting out of it.''

"Turn off the lights, Miss Wilson. We are going to dinner.''

Meekly, Abbey obeyed.

The Scarpinos greeted Abbey like the long-lost and favorite daughter of the family. Mama Scarpino showed them to the best corner table farthest away from the kitchen. Much whispering in the kitchen caused several dark-eyed faces topped with curly dark hair to peek out of the swinging door. Gabe peered at her over the gigantic menu.

"You seem to be well known here,'' he stated as water, antipasto and bread appeared like magic on the checkered tablecloth.

"I was the maid of honor for Gina's wedding. That's their oldest. We spent many happy hours making delicious goodies in the kitchen under Mama's supervision. Mama's American food is terrific, but her Italian specialties are really outstanding.'' Abbey laughed.

Several people stopped by on their way out of the restaurant to greet Abbey and Gabe. As their rigatoni arrived, the place seemed to empty. Gabe regarded her with some amusement.

"I don't suppose there's any place in this town that you are inconspicuous?''

Abbey shrugged philosophically. "No, I don't think so. You can look at it in two ways. Either you live in a very small town, or you have an exceedingly large family. I prefer the second point of view. Eat your pasta. Mama has a stricken look on her face. You're supposed to dig in and look overcome with delight.''

They proceeded to do just that. After a while Gabe's face wore a look of wonder as he raised his head from his plate. He was smiling rapturously.

"This is the best Italian food I've ever tasted, and I've eaten in some of the better restaurants in Chicago and New York. This is the best. I'm amazed!"

Abbey noticed that Mama's plump face was wreathed in smiles. She had observed Gabe's reaction. It was good to see the thin man across from her chase a piece of rigatoni with a fork. Mama's cooking could do wonders for the hollows below those cheekbones.

She was glad to see his usual tension overcome by the warmth of the Scarpino family and the good food. Gabe leaned back while she finished her food at a more leisurely pace. Over coffee and spumoni he relaxed even more, discussing the upcoming changeover to the soup line.

"We know we have a good market for the apple products. It remains to be seen if we can capture the public with the home soup line. My father firmly believes that we'll be successful with it. I'm willing to be convinced."

Abbey agreed with the elder Kendall. "I'm glad your father is taking such an interest in the factory," she remarked. "My father told me about his heart attack. Dad has left several messages at the house, but they haven't been answered."

Gabe's eyes took on a shuttered appearance. "It would be difficult for Dad to be around an old friend who would remind him of happier times."

"My father has also suffered a severe loss," Abbey reminded him. "They might be able to comfort each other."

His eyes now reflected the glitter of the flickering candle

flame on their table. "I don't think my father needs to hear a lot of sentimental drivel about accepting his fate unquestioningly. You have no idea how trying you do-gooders can be."

"Ouch!" murmured Abbey succinctly.

"We'll get along just fine if you stay out of my personal life, Miss Wilson," Gabe warned. "Neither my father nor I need anyone mucking around in our private affairs." Gabe signaled an older Scarpino child for the check.

Outside the little restaurant, Abbey stopped beside the car. "If you don't mind, Mr. Kendall, I'll walk home. It's only two blocks to the rectory, and it's a beautiful night."

"I'll take you home, Miss Wilson, if you don't mind."

Abbey was losing patience. She didn't want to get into an enclosed space with this irritated man. "I do mind, sir," she said formally. "Thank you for the dinner, but I prefer to walk home under my own power."

Abbey started walking. Much to her dismay, she found a tall figure pacing beside her. She felt ridiculous, taking three steps to his one. They walked the first block in silence until she halted at the corner and looked up at him accusingly.

He glared back. "In my family it is the custom to see a dinner partner home safely. I'll accompany you to your door, Miss Wilson, whether you walk, hop or skip all the way to your house. Is that clear?"

"Perfectly," she said calmly and continued walking. This was dreadful. Frantically she tried to think of a way to save the sinking evening. He was right. She should mind her own business.

She was relieved when the old church loomed up in the darkness. Stubbornly he followed her to the rectory walk and up the front steps. She was overjoyed to see her father sitting on the porch swing.

"Dad," she yelped happily. "I called, but you were out. Did you have dinner?"

Ira looked a little confused at her overzealous greeting, but he answered equably. "I had dinner out, my dear. How are you, Gabe? I hope everything is going well for you."

"Thank you, Mr. Wilson," Gabe answered coolly. "The cannery is doing quite well. We're starting the second line at the end of this month."

"Yes," Ira continued, "your father was telling me about that this afternoon. He has great hopes for the line on a national basis."

"You saw my father?" Gabe rasped. "He's not supposed to be bothered by visitors."

"I didn't think that included old friends," Ira reproved gently. "We had a fine afternoon talking over old times. He's really pleased with the renovation of the Johnson place. That picture window in his room is spectacular, isn't it?"

"Normally my father rests in the afternoons," Gabe answered. "The doctors have recommended that he lead a quiet life free of any anxiety."

"It's interesting how you young people think a quiet life should be no life at all," countered Ira firmly. "Your father was lonely, Gabe. He needs to get out of the house and see friends. This weekend I'm taking him to a chess tournament at the recreation hall. Ralph used to be an excellent player, and there's nothing wrong with his right arm. He'll enjoy an afternoon of chess. If he tires, I'll bring him home."

"I don't think that will be possible," Gabe stated coldly.

"I think you'd better ask your father about that," advised Ira. "It really is his choice, isn't it?"

The two men held each other's eyes for a moment. Gabe turned abruptly and stalked down the steps and away without another word. Abbey dropped into the swing beside her father.

"You see what I mean, Dad? Everything I do seems to upset that man. I don't know who he was maddest at, you or me."

"Abbey," Ira commented sadly, "he's angry at the world. Mostly he's angry at the Lord for what happened to him."

"What can we do?" Abbey cried.

"Just what I told you before," Ira chided. "Pray and have faith. The Lord will work it out. It's too complicated for us, but it's nothing for Him."

"I know you're right," Abbey agreed. "My heart keeps getting in the way of my head."

Ira patted her on the head. "There are worse sins." He got up and started inside to escape the chilly November evening. "Oh, by the way, we have two more guests for Thanksgiving dinner."

Abbey followed him. "Oh? Who?"

"Ralph and Gabe Kendall." Ira went into the house, leaving a stunned Abbey to trail after him.

She followed him through the house and into the kitchen. "Dad, how did you manage that? Gabe Kendall will never allow it. How did you even get to see Ralph Kendall?"

Ira poured some cocoa he'd been heating on the stove into a cup and sat down at the kitchen table. "Actually, it was that nice Mrs. Strickler's idea. It was a good one, too.

She and I went over to the house together. While she kept the nurse busy at the front door, I went in the back door.''

"Dad, they could have had you arrested for breaking and entering," Abbey moaned.

"Nonsense. When I went upstairs, I found Ralph just sitting there, staring out that marvelous window. The nurse discovered me, of course, but Ralph overruled her. We had a pleasant afternoon. It was hardest on Mrs. Strickler. She spent the entire three hours waiting for me in the car. She's an exceptional person, don't you think?"

"Lesley is a darling, but you were both crazy. Glory! It might have cost both Lesley and me our jobs!"

"Ralph was very happy to see me. After all, he moved here because he had always loved visiting us. As for losing your jobs, please remember that Ralph is a partner in the cannery. He doesn't need to be, of course. He made a lot of money when they sold the conglomerate off, but he needed some interest in life. His son was making everything so easy that there was nothing left for Ralph to do. That's the worst thing you can do to men of our age. You tend to do a little of that, too, young lady."

Abbey looked guilty. "It's just that we want things to be better for our parents, Dad. I'm sure Gabe Kendall is only trying to do the best for his father. You are all the family we both have. We want to give you a little of all you've given us."

"That's fine, dear." Ira patted her hand. "Just try to remember that we should have the choice of how we want help. We really don't need it stuffed down our throats like those vitamin pills you keep making me take."

Abbey looked at the dear, fragile features and almost wept. She hadn't realized she was being so overprotective.

"Both you and Gabe need to be aware of the fact that Ralph and I are the fathers. We do not take well to being treated like children. If we need help, we'll ask for it. I promise you, I will ask. We're more concerned that our children's lives are being crippled because of us."

"That's not true," said Abbey stoutly.

"Isn't it?" Ira spoke softly. "Then why aren't you in Chicago working at that job you loved so much? Isn't it because you felt you couldn't abandon this old man?"

Abbey had the grace to blush.

"Abbey," Ira said sternly, "when I needed you to help with your mother, I called you, didn't I? Why do you think I'll fade away without your being here? I'm not saying I don't enjoy having you home. You know I do, but you're making me feel very guilty. Gabe is doing the same thing to Ralph. He didn't need to sell out all of his holdings to stay with his father. With competent assistants, Ralph could have run the cannery from his office."

"Dad"—Abbey's eyes brimmed over—"it's because we love you so much."

Ira was very moved by Abbey's tears, but he felt that it was her love for him that kept her away from a good career and marriage. "Love is free, Abbey. When it destroys part of another, it becomes selfishness, not love. Please think about this. A good parent is happiest when his child is fulfilled. I don't want to be the cause of your losing your chance at real happiness." He kissed her good night and went to bed.

Alone, Abbey sat in the kitchen with her thoughts. What she had been critical of in Gabe, she was guilty of herself. A knock on the back door interrupted her reverie. She opened it to the object of her thoughts.

Gabe handed her the pair of gloves she had left in his car. "I thought you might need these. The mornings are cold now."

"Thank you," she said in some confusion. "And please accept my apologies. You were absolutely right. I have no business interfering in your private life."

"That's all right," he said sardonically. "It seems to be a family failing."

"Would you like some hot chocolate?" she offered.

"No, not tonight," he said politely. "You seem to dish out advice with food. I've had my quota for the day."

As he started to leave, she called out gaily, "I'll see you for Thanksgiving dinner." She closed the door on his outraged "What?"

For some reason her heart felt lighter and a bubbling laugh rose to her lips. If the Lord was going to take care of everything, Abbey might as well enjoy the process.

Chapter Four

W ould you mind if I just laid my head on my plate and took a nap?'' Amy moaned. "I'm too full to make it to the living room sofa."

"I'd carry you," Ross offered kindly, "but I don't have the strength. Abbey worked me so hard all morning that I barely managed to eat all five helpings of turkey."

Abbey joined the laughter. "Our plates are yours. Feel free. After the wonderful job you all did helping with the dinner today, you deserve a reward."

"I think I've been overrewarded," groaned Lesley. "Anyway, it was fun. Abbey is the one who deserves the rest. Not only did she organize the dinner for everyone at the church, but she was sprinting back and forth preparing our dinner, too!"

"It helped me work up an appetite," Abbey assured her.

"If it weren't for the cannery," Ira inserted, "there

would have been a great many more needy people and less food. Those baskets of goodies Ralph and Gabe provided for the people to take home were a thoughtful gift.''

"That was a wonderful idea." Abbey smiled into the dark blue eyes of the man on her right. Even in a wheelchair, Ralph Kendall was a distinguished gentleman. "I saw you talking to some of our local chess champions, Mr. Kendall.''

"I thought I was a good chess player until I tangled with some of those fellows." His smile lit up the strong features. "Ira and I need a good deal more practice before being a threat to them, don't we?''

"You were always better at thinking ahead than I," Ira retorted. "I was never much of a chess player, but I'm a killer at Chinese checkers. I'll take you on later.''

"I haven't played that since I was a kid." Emil Eisen considered a dollop of cranberry sauce on his plate. "Amy was never one for games. She always misplaced the marbles.''

"That's because Dad was so mean when he lost," Amy teased. "It was easier to lose the checkers, marbles or dice than to get into an argument. Never play Monopoly with a banker. They forget it's a game.''

"We'll join you in the living room after the dishes are done," Lesley said cheerfully.

"Can we help?" Gabe Kendall had said so little at the table that his voice startled Abbey.

"The best help you men can be is to stay out of our way." Lesley chuckled.

It was fun to share work in the kitchen again, thought Abbey. She had missed the old camaraderie of women working together in her home since the death of her mother.

Lesley washed, Amy dried and Abbey put the dishes away. The pleasant rumble of male voices floated in from the living room.

Lesley and Amy were joking about letting out the strings of the aprons Abbey had found for them. "How can it feel so good to eat too much?" complained Amy.

The day had gone well for everyone. Abbey had started at 5 A.M., when she and Mama Scarpino met to stuff the turkeys and put them in the church ovens for the dinner for the elderly and indigent of Counsel. The rest of the group had arrived at 9 A.M. to set the tables and unfold wooden chairs. Gabe and Ross had done all of the heavy work. Then they had charmed the guests by helping to serve the food. Ralph Kendall had joined several of the men from the retirement home and chattered happily. Abbey had noticed Millicent Shriers talking at length to Gabe over her pie. Amy, of course, was her usual lovely self in her stunning wheat-colored dress of wool crepe. Even Abbey had indulged in a new rust jersey that brought out the shine in her chestnut hair and made her brown eyes sparkle. Millicent had remarked that the two A's looked like the spirit of autumn.

Amy had stopped Abbey briefly in a corner and asked for an introduction to Ross. "I tried to charm your boss, Abbey. Honestly, it's like trying to warm up a fish in a tank. You can't get through the glass barrier. Who is the tall one with the topaz eyes? He looks about as comfortable in the kitchen as I do in the office."

Amy and Ross were duly introduced and seemed to hit it off immediately. Abbey had to admit that she had never thought of Ross's light brown eyes as being "topaz." Obviously Amy noticed more about Ross than she had. He was nice, but Abbey had thought that Gabe would be much more interesting to her friend than his young assistant. Ross was something of a flirt; Gabe had so much more substance. Abbey shook her head. Occasionally her friend's taste disappointed her.

Amy was pumping Lesley about Ross while she dried the dishes. Lesley's gray eyes sparkled. "I'll tell you this, Amy. If anyone is a match for Ross Ellis, it might be you. He's escaped feminine nets for years. You've got to understand that he isn't really happy in Counsel. He feels that the people here don't like him."

"Then," said Amy with a sly grin, "he needs to meet the right people."

Lesley had apparently gotten over her antipathy to Amy, for which Abbey was grateful. She wanted her friends to be friends. Amy was really at her best when she was charming a group, as she had at the dinner. Abbey sighed contentedly. She loved making people happy. Even Gabe had smiled often throughout the day. What a difference it made to his features!

The woman laid the pie and coffee out on the dining room table. It was too soon for dessert, but it would be there when they were ready for it.

"Aha!" yelped Ross. "Rescue is at hand! Quick, Lesley. They were about to commandeer me for a game of checkers."

Ira looked hopefully at Abbey. "It's more fun when there are six players."

"But we still need a sixth." Abbey looked at Amy.

"A fate worse than death," trilled Amy, settling on the sofa next to Ross.

"Get over here, Gabe," commanded Ralph. "Uphold the Kendall pride."

Gabe drowsily declined, but was overruled by his father. Shaking his head, he took his place across from Abbey at the round table.

"I'm going to play the blue marbles," announced Emil, who was sitting across from Ralph. "My blue marbles always win."

"Not against my green," threatened Ralph.

"Do I have to play with purple?" Gabe got into the spirit of the fun.

"You can have my red, if you don't jump my marbles for the first three turns," offered Abbey.

"Never," said Gabe dryly. "I'll play the purple."

"White always goes first," said Ira, suiting actions to words.

"I never heard of that rule," protested Ralph.

"It's his game," Lesley added.

All afternoon they played the ridiculous game. A minister, a banker, two executives, an executive secretary and an assistant laughed, squabbled and bantered over the table. Amy and Ross shouted encouragement from the sidelines.

At the end they were weak from laughing. Lesley had outfoxed them all and won six of the seven games.

"I have nieces and nephews," she explained modestly.

"It was the purple marbles," Gabe defended himself. "Who could win with purple?"

"No one," quipped Ralph, "when they keep picking up the wrong marbles to jump with."

"Psychologically I was rejecting the purple," Gabe said complacently.

"That's a wonderful excuse," Abbey complimented him.

"I thought so." Gabe chuckled.

Abbey smiled into his eyes and was startled by the Prussian-blue sparkle. She had never seen his eyes so alive, and her mouth almost dropped open from shock. He noticed her bemused look.

"Ah, Abbey," Gabe said gently, "you are pouring that coffee onto the tablecloth."

"Oh!" Abbey looked at the brimming cup.

Gabe removed the coffeepot from her hand as she fell into an attack of helpless giggles.

"Here, you two." Lesley rescued the pot from Gabe. "People who can't handle the excitement of Chinese checkers should abstain from them."

Ross observed the merriment from the sofa with Amy. "It reminds me of the good old days. We used to laugh a lot."

Amy said softly, "If anyone could help that unhappy man, it would be Abbey. She's practically a walking first-aid station for broken spirits."

"You do a lot to lift the old ego yourself, young lady," Ross said gallantly. "I didn't think I'd make even one friend in this town, other than Abbey and her father."

"That's what I mean about Abbey. She has a lot of friends. For some of those people, she's their only friend. She's a great deal like her mother, although she looks more like Ira. The Wilson family is the soul of Counsel."

"You look pretty good to me," complimented Ross.

Amy's eyes flickered a warning signal, but Ross continued on with his flattering patter until he realized she wasn't responding.

"I am deafened by your silence." He gave her a puzzled look. "I could have sworn we were friends a moment ago. I feel a distinct chill coming on."

"I do like you," Amy admitted.

"I'm relieved." Ross heaved a sigh.

"So I'm going to tell you the truth."

"Uh-oh."

"You keep saying you have no friends here. Why haven't you tried to figure out the reason for that instead of comdemning the town?"

Ross was caught by surprise. "I thought they just didn't like big-city people."

"Do you really believe that?" Amy's eyes were clear and inquisitive.

Ross had the feeling that their future relationship hung on his answer, but the truth was more painful that he wanted to admit. On the other hand, losing this lovely woman's friendship might be more painful than the truth.

"No. No, I don't."

"What do you think is the reason?" Amy persisted.

Ross's face took on the look of a bewildered fox. "They just don't like me."

Amy's heart went out to the man who had answered her honestly. "Had you gone to Abbey, Ira, me or anyone else in the town with that truth, we would have willingly helped you. We would have explained to you why your approach is so irritating."

"Thanks." Ross's body stiffened.

"I don't want to hurt you. I'm trying to help you." Amy touched his hand.

"It's hard to tell the difference."

"I know. I really do know. When I came back home a

year ago, I found the town very cold. Abbey helped me realize where the problem was.''

"I don't see how you could have any problem being liked," Ross insisted.

"It's that kind of meaningless nonsense that does it. You're so busy impressing, you aren't listening. Your patter is so rehearsed that it's mere drivel. You're good at it, Ross, but in Counsel it is spotted for what it really is—uncaring noise.''

"Funny." Ross sounded hurt. "I've been pretty success-ful for a bag of 'uncaring noise,' which I assume is a euphemism for 'a bag of wind.'"

"I mean," Amy continued carefully, "that here you are judged by your sincerity, honesty and industry. How clever you are with your tongue is not considered a winning trait. You had some trouble with the Davis family because they sensed you were condescending to them. Maybe Zeb Davis didn't impress you in his overalls with manure on his boots, but his farm sits on a million dollars' worth of land. Can you say the same? We don't judge people by the cut of their suit here. We judge them by their nobility of spirit.''

"You're straight out of *Pilgrim's Progress*," snapped Ross in spite of himself.

"No I'm not," Amy corrected him. "You and I are alike in some ways. Let me put it like this. You talked about how sad Gabe is, but what did you do about it?''

Ross looked confused.

"Look at him, Ross. You see, Abbey knew what to do. Ira knew how to help Ralph. They don't talk about helping—they help. You say to yourself that you didn't know what to do. With all of your success in business, you couldn't help one friend. You don't know how to help anyone else. I didn't either. Abbey hardly knows Gabe, but she knows what his spirit needs.''

"Maybe it's because I'm a city boy," suggested a hopeful Ross.

"Poor excuse." Amy was unrelenting. "The Scarpinos came to us from Chicago, and they're loved by everyone in Counsel.''

"Excuse me," said Ross. "I think it's time for me to go home and mourn my lost ego.''

"I like you," reiterated Amy. "That's why I'm telling you this.''

Ross rose and looked down at the silvery hair that haloed Amy's head. "Do me a favor, Miss Eisen. Don't like me anymore. I think I would have been better off if you didn't like me.''

Abbey was serving the pumpkin pie when Ross took his leave. "Ross, aren't you going to stay for pie?''

Ross's eyes had a peculiar look. "I've already had more than enough. Thanks for all the goodies, Abbey.''

"You aren't angry for having to work at the dinner all morning, are you?''

Ross patted her shoulder. "From what I hear, it may have been the only good thing I've done in this town. No, I really enjoyed helping.'' He made his good-byes to the group, retrieved his coat and left.

Gabe's eyes met Abbey's as they both watched Ross leave. Amy wandered over to them, looking desolate.

"What happened to Ross?'' asked Abbey. "You seemed to be having fun.''

"He just got his first inoculation to Counsel." Amy's voice sounded slightly hollow. "It gives some people a strong reaction.''

"I beg your pardon?" inquired Gabe.

Amy sighed. "I may have made the dosage a little too strong."

Abbey said softly, "Oh, Amy."

Gabe was now thoroughly confused. "I have the feeling that my father needs another cup of coffee."

Abbey put her arm around her friend's shoulder after Gabe's quick exit.

"Abbey, I really liked him." Amy's expression was woebegone.

Abbey understood what Ross had not. She bit her lip. It was so rare for Amy to let down her defenses. She hoped that Ross Ellis was not a mistake for Amy. She looked at her friend's rueful face.

"Don't worry. It will work out." She prayed that she was right.

Everyone left together, with Emil giving Lesley a lift to her house. Just as they were saying their farewells, great white flakes started drifting down.

Ralph Kendall looked up into the snow and tasted it. "Now, that makes the day perfect. Look at the size of those flakes!"

"Come now, Ralph," mocked Emil. "You certainly had snow in Chicago!"

Ralph's lion features took on a look of wonder. "Of course we did, but I never noticed it. Here I can see the individual flakes."

"We'd better get going," said Gabe. "Those individual flakes combine to make slippery roads."

Gabe shook Ira's hand. "Thank you for a great day." He smiled up at Abbey. "Thanks for everything."

Abbey and Ira waved to them from the porch. The sound

of "Jingle Bells" drifted back to them from the Eisen car. In her mind, Abbey kept seeing that commanding face with the soft snowflakes catching on his eyelashes. How warm and beautiful his voice sounded when he was happy. She had once wondered what Gabe Kendall had been like before the accident. Now she knew she had just had a small glimpse of it. Her heart turned over in empathy for the kind of man he had been.

The next few days were busy with the factory changeover to the soup line. They were all run a little ragged. Now Abbey was dealing with the farmers and meat packing houses for the vegetables and meats that went into the soups. Ross was frequently out of town for days at a time making arrangements for the distributors and the advertising campaigns.

The Iowa Nobles products had been a great success. Both Gabe and Ralph were happy with the proceeds. Deliveries were going out every day from the storehouses as new orders poured in.

Gabe, Lesley and Abbey spent several evenings at the cannery eating carry-out food from Scarpino's restaurant.

Everything was on schedule, but that didn't stop Gabe from putting in longer hours than anyone else. Ralph complained to Ira that he might as well live alone in the big old house except for the nurse, whom he resented mightily.

Ross was back, and the executive staff was sharing another of Mama Scarpino's meals after an evening session. They had been discussing the new transportation arrangements for the soups. Ross had been throwing out times, schedules and statistics until Lesley pleaded for a rest to digest her meal.

''We can't eat figures with spaghetti,'' she insisted. ''Take a break, Ross.''

After Thanksgiving, Gabe seemed to have returned to his old ways, but now even he remonstrated. ''Take it easy, Ross—you'll burn yourself out before the deadline. I know your figures are correct. They always are.''

Ross shut his mouth with a snap and attacked his food silently. The other three looked at one another and then at Ross. They said nothing until he looked up from his plate.

''What's the matter?''

''We might ask you that question,'' ventured Lesley. ''For the last week or so, you've been running around here like an old-time movie. I can't keep up with you.''

''That's me,'' said Ross bitterly. ''Efficient, hardworking, brilliant as a worker but a dead loss as a person.''

Gabe's eyebrows went up. He had never seen his assistant in this kind of mood. ''I think we'd better stop for tonight.''

''Not on my account,'' said Ross. ''I'm sorry. I guess I'm irritable because of the new line. I'll behave myself.''

''What on earth makes you think you're a loss as a person?'' Abbey asked, getting to the heart of the matter.

''This town,'' said Ross.

''The whole town has attacked you?'' asked Gabe.

''Let us say, it's not my kind of life,'' Ross stated glumly.

Lesley was quick to defend her adopted home. ''What chance have you given the town?''

''What chance has it given me?''

''You did very well at the Thanksgiving dinner,'' Abbey reminded him.

''Sure, I'm not too bad with elderly people, especially

when we're giving them free food. Who wouldn't be popular in that setting?''

Lesley thought a minute. ''Mr. Eisen and his daughter seemed to like you.''

Ross leveled a look at her. ''Right. The way goldfish like barracuda.''

Abbey knew what had brought this on, and she felt a glimmer of joy for Amy. If Ross hadn't cared what Amy thought, he wouldn't be so upset. There was more to Ross than she had realized, but she didn't want him to give up and leave town before Amy had her chance.

''I think you're wrong,'' Lesley said. ''Amy really likes you.''

''I *know* you're wrong,'' Abbey said.

''Pardon me, Abbey,'' Ross said tiredly, ''you like everyone. If Jack the Ripper lived here, you and your father would get up a collection to send him to a mental health facility.''

Gabe was drinking some water and nearly choked. When he could breathe, he leaned back and laughed until tears ran down his cheeks.

The other three stared at him in utter astonishment.

''I'm glad my problem amuses you,'' commented Ross.

''No. It's just that you certainly put Abbey in a nutshell.'' Gabe gasped for air and tried to control himself. ''The image of Abbey taking up a cause was so real.''

''I'm glad it amuses you that I care,'' Abbey reproved him.

''I'm glad you're all glad,'' fumed Ross.

That set everyone off again into gales of laughter, with Ross relunctantly joining in. ''Ah,'' he said, ''I guess I was taking myself too seriously. I have too much time to think when I'm here. In the city, if I get the blues, I take off and go somewhere with someone. Here I can walk the streets at night and meet all of the neighborhood animals or talk to the raccoons in the park. The conversations tend to be one-sided. I even had a Great Dane reject me last night. He found a cocker spaniel more interesting company.''

"I had no idea you were in such dire straits." Gabe looked at his assistant with some concern. "Personally I find that the local cats like to gossip over the fence around midnight.''

Abbey was amazed that Gabe had the sense to respond to Ross's problem with a light touch. Except for Thanksgiving, she would not have believed that he had a sense of humor.

Lesley was smiling at the two men like the proverbial mother hen. "In a small town you have to make your own entertainment, gentlemen. You have dinners, breakfasts and open houses. You join the business club. Most of the events here are in private homes. However, Ross, what you need to do is get on the phone and call a certain lady and ask her out to dinner so that the rest of us can live with you.''

"I don't know what you're talking about." Ross began to shred his untouched salad into tiny bits.

"She's talking about Amy Eisen, who assumed you would call her to continue your Thanksgiving conversation and is very disappointed." Abbey took Ross's fork away from him so that he had to look at her. "She liked you well enough to be honest with you, and you took your marbles and went home in a huff.''

"So that's what this is all about." Gabe looked relieved. "I thought you were having some kind of an identity crisis.''

"That's precisely what I am having. That delicate Dresden doll nearly took me apart and left me to bleed all over the place."

"Nonsense," Lesley insisted. "You ran away to lick your wounds before she got the chance to bind them up."

Ross's face lightened. "I thought she was trying to get rid of me."

Abbey gave Ross back his fork. "If Amy had wanted to lose you, you would be gone, Ross. She likes you. Now eat your dinner so that you'll have the strength to ask her for a date."

Ross dipped into the salad that was now a slaw and munched. "Yes, ma'am!"

Lesley finished her dinner and went off to complete some schedules, and Ross exited to make a certain phone call. Abbey was left alone with her boss.

"If you've solved the problems of the lovelorn, perhaps we might get down to that checklist." Gabe pulled a sheaf of papers over to him.

Abbey looked at him through her eyelashes for signs of irritation. She was pleased to see a smile tugging at the corners of his mouth. He glanced up and caught her looking at him.

"I'm not quite the monster you seem to think me, Abbey." He grinned at her. "Even I could see that Amy Eisen and Ross were attracted to each other."

"You don't mind?"

"First of all, the personal lives of my employees are none of my business; a belief that *some of my employees* don't seem to have about my life." Abbey blushed.

"Second, married men make better employees. They tend to work harder, with fewer distractions. Third, I am fully aware that the lovely Miss Eisen was being thrown at my head initially. It was creating a situation that could be potentially uncomfortable for both of us. I have never been a butterfly collector. That particular lady scares me to death.''

Abbey came to the defense of her friend. ''Amy is not a butterfly! She's a warm, generous, kindhearted friend. She is also a leader here and could do her husband a great deal of good.''

''Deliver me from managing women,'' sighed Gabe.

''Excuse me, Mr. Kendall. I have found that most men are managed by their women. It's just a matter of finding out what kind of woman you want to be managed by. Amy is a subtle, beautiful woman.''

''Would you put yourself in that category?''

Abbey's blush deepened. ''No, sir. I know that I'm not beautiful or subtle, but I won't see Amy condemned because those are her gifts.''

''I wasn't aware I was condemning her. I was merely stating that she was not for me. Why do you sell yourself short? Are you not as beautiful as Miss Eisen? There are many men who prefer the rose to the orchid. One of the reasons I hesitated about hiring you was that you were too attractive. I was afraid you would marry one of your gallant admirers and leave me in the lurch.''

His courtly speech so flummoxed Abbey that she was speechless. She had firmly believed that he saw her only as an extension of his business arm. It hadn't occurred to her that he saw her as a person in her own right. They seemed to work so well together, but nearly every social encounter caused friction. Every day she had to readjust her perceptions of this man. It was all very confusing.

Her confusion must have shown in her face, for he continued. "I believe in marriage. I had a very happy one myself. Even though that's over for me, I would certainly recommend it to others. Contrary to popular opinion, I don't want anyone else to suffer a loss simply because I must live with mine."

Frozen, Abbey watched the pain creep into those blue eyes. "Some of us are only allowed the spring season of loving. My father knew all four seasons, but I wasn't so lucky. Excuse me, I think we'll finish this a little later."

His anguish so filled the room that Abbey reached out a hand to touch his sleeve. "Sir, you do realize that spring comes back each year. The heart is capable of unlimited loving. We do not love those we have lost any less by loving again."

"Not for me, Abbey." He turned away. "However, I have one request of you."

"Anything."

"Could you please stop calling me 'sir'? It makes me feel like a particularly irascible headmaster! 'Gabe' will do."

"Yes, sir—Gabe . . ."

"Practice. You'll get it."

"I'll write it five hundred times on the blackboard."

She was rewarded when a deep chuckle rumbled from his chest. "I can see why the Wilsons ran this town for generations."

"Actually, we didn't run it," said Abbey modestly. "The people ran it, and still do. We just let them believe we ran it. They feel better when they have someone else to blame for mistakes."

This time he laughed and turned back to her. "I believe I have taken a viper to my bosom."

"More like you have given room to a garter snake, but we're good for gardens."

Ross popped in briefly. "She said yes."

"Of course," said Gabe and Abbey in unison.

Ross blinked and popped out.

Lesley appeared with another stack of schedules and they settled down to work. Abbey was pleased with the few moments she and Gabe had shared. He might not like Amy, but there were other girls in town. There was hope for Gabe yet. The Lord was obviously working on the man. His defenses were crumbling. Any woman who had met him in the last half hour could not help but find him attractive. Those blue eyes against that light skin were startling; when he smiled, he was devastating. She watched his strong fingers sort lists in front of him. The arm under her hand had been equally powerful. She shivered without knowing why and bent her head to the lists.

They were on the last page, checking and rechecking, when Ross appeared in the doorway. His silence caught their attention. His face telegraphed trouble.

"We have problems," Ross blurted. "Big ones."

Chapter Five

Slumped in his chair, Ross explained how he had received a phone call from Chicago. The fleet of trucks that were to take the soups to Chicago on Monday were unavailable. The recent death of the owner had thrown the company into receivership. The drivers had been locked out until some kind of financial and tax mess could be sorted out.

"It'll take time to make arrangements for another line to take over, and time is something we don't have!" Ross ran shaky fingers through his hair.

"We'll get on the phone tomorrow and explain the situation to our distributors. They'll understand. It's happened before." Gabe's voice was a flat monotone.

Ross's face was a study in misery. "Our credibility will suffer if we can't even deliver our first shipment on schedule."

Gabe put his hand on Ross's shoulder. "This could have

happened to anyone. You've done your best, Ross. You're not responsible for the problem. Let's just handle it the best way we can.''

Abbey was impressed by Gabe's generosity. This was a terrible blow for a new product. The last two days of work had just gone down the drain. No matter what Gabe had said to Ross, they all knew that some distributors would get upset and cause trouble. Abbey's sympathy went out to Ross, who was so obviously suffering, just as her heart went out to Gabe, who did not allow his disappointment to show.

"Let's shut down for the night," Gabe suggested. "We're all too tired to think clearly. We'll draft a battle plan in the morning. Get some sleep, Ross. No one can do better than their best.''

Abbey, Lesley and Ross stood in the parking lot looking up at the light in the window of Gabe's office. Lesley shook her head sadly. "He sends us home, but you notice that he's still working.''

Ross leaned against his car in mute misery.

"You couldn't have foreseen the man's death, Ross," Abbey insisted. "Stop blaming yourself. Gabe was right. No one could have known.''

"I should have checked up earlier this week. I let my emotional life interfere with my professional obligations.''

"Would that have changed the results?" asked Abbey.

"We might have had more warning," Ross said glumly.

"If only we could do something to help!" Lesley exclaimed.

"If only the town could help him as he has helped the town." Abbey looked up at the lonely window and thought of the man behind it.

"If wishes were pennies, we'd all be rich." Ross opened the car door. "Come on, ladies. I'll drop you off."

Abbey sat in the backseat while Lesley and Ross carried on a desultory conversation. Silently she prayed for the Lord to help them. She knew that there was a reason for everything in His will. She prayed that they could solve this to everyone's benefit, even though it was hard to see a benefit from this situation. She prayed for understanding.

They stopped at Abbey's house. Ross opened the door and looked at Abbey's concerned expression. "Tuck in a prayer or two for me tonight," he begged. "It's a shame this had to happen, but that's the kind of problem you have in a small town with few resources."

Oh, Ross, thought Abbey to herself, you don't see the resources in this town because you don't know our greatest resource—the people. Gabe saw that. Why can't you? She started away from the car and stopped. That was it! Why hadn't she thought of it before?

Lesley and Ross were astonished at the joyous look on Abbey's face. "I've got it! You made me think of it, Ross! Come in, quickly. We've got a lot of work to do."

Ross didn't believe in the plan at first, but, with Ira's help, Abbey and Lesley convinced him. When Abbey called Amy to come and help man the phone brigade, Ross threw up his hands and gave in.

The next morning Ross called Gabe and informed him that they had found a new trucking line to take the soups to Chicago. Gabe was somewhat mystified about the transportation, but relieved. He threw himself into the logistics of packing and scheduling, leaving the transportation to Ross and Abbey.

Gabe was kept busy in the factory and was unaware of

the changes. The first thing he noticed was his father firmly ensconced in his office with Ira acting as his assistant. They both merrily waved him to the dock where the loading was taking place. He walked out onto the platform and froze. From in front of the dock and down the road as far as the eye could see were trucks, vans and cars. He could see the apple trucks from the farms, the Payne Grocery Store van, the Scarpinos' panel truck, and his factory foreman's family camper, with the man's wife at the wheel. Everyone waved at him.

Abbey smiled up at him with her clipboard full of lists. "How do you like the Counsel Trucking Service?"

"It's not possible."

"Oh yes. Don't worry. Ross, Lesley and I worked it all out. Everyone has maps and knows where to go. It may surprise the distributors to see our fleet, but the product will be on time. Your dad and mine are calling the distributors right now."

Bemused, Gabe waved back at a chubby hand that was pumping up and down from a station wagon window. "Is the whole town here?"

Ross appeared on his other side. "Just about everyone who isn't working in the factory." He waved at Amy, who was sitting in the cab of a rental truck. "Isn't she fantastic? Who would have believed she could drive a truck?"

Abbey smiled proudly at the thunderstruck Gabe. "They wanted to show you how much they cared. Not a single person we called refused to help."

As if mesmerized, Gabe's eyes followed the long line. His hand went up as though to brush the sight from his eyes, and then he looked again. Still Abbey and Ross caught the telltale brightness in his eyes.

"We will have to pay for the gas, of course." Ross studied his clipboard.

"Of course." Gabe's voice had a strangled sound.

"It would be nice if you spoke to them as they loaded," Abbey suggested, urging him gently toward the volunteers.

Gabe's eyes were a bright, shiny blue as he smiled at her. "Well, let's not keep our people waiting!"

Abbey almost sat down in the middle of the dock from sheer relief. Her legs were definitely wobbly, and her heart was pounding. Was she having an anxiety attack after the fact? She had an irresistible urge to throw her arms around Gabe Kendall and embrace him in front of the entire town. She was more tired than she realized. She followed his broad back down the steps toward the waiting crowd.

She was so pleased with the way he handled each person. He gravely accepted a sucker from the chubby hand in the station wagon, even though it was already half-licked. He shook Zeb's hand and accepted a bottle of red cider from Emma. He laughed when Mama Scarpino gave him a large, smacking kiss, and joked with the five members of the Bailey clan. By afternoon the last elderly pickup had trundled down the road to make the eight-hour trip to Chicago. Ross had left with Amy to head up the delivery to the largest distributor.

Abbey felt very small on the large dock. Although the wind was cold and biting, she felt curiously warm. Gabe turned from watching the last truck disappear down the road with his eyes still that glowing, bright blue. Abbey leaned against the brick wall of the building. She sighed with relief. They had done it. Ross had made all the arrangements for the rest of the deliveries that season with professional carriers. Their copybook would be free of blots as far as the distributors were concerned. She shivered, wishing Ross had not taken off in the general exodus. Gabe had been gracious to the townspeople. After all, what could he do? She remembered the liberties she had taken with the dishes at his house. What if he was really angry about their plans? He would never have shown it in so public a place, but now she was all alone. She started edging toward the door, but he caught her hands. All of her uncertainties came to the surface and she hung her head.

"I realize that we took a lot for granted," she stammered. "I thought it was a perfect solution because it gave the townspeople a chance to show you how grateful they are for everything you've done for them." She knew she was chattering, but she couldn't stop and couldn't look up into those eyes. His large hands had completely enveloped hers. "It's not the most conventional means, but it was an emergency."

He cut across her nervous flow easily. "Your hands are cold. Don't you ever wear gloves, or have you lost them?"

She looked up into those deep blue eyes and was lost. "It's hard to mark a checklist when I'm wearing gloves." Her voice was faint because she felt the peculiar sensation she had felt earlier.

He put his arm around her and pulled her against his side. "You are cold."

Oh no, she thought. I'm warm. Much too warm.

"It was a wonderful idea," Gabe said. "I'm beginning to realize just how terrific the people in this town are. My father was right about moving here."

His arm tightened and Abbey had to remind herself to breathe. She could feel the strength of those broad shoulders and wanted above all to put her arms around him. Her hands clutched the clipboard. He pressed a quick, warm kiss against her mouth, and released her.

"Thank you." He opened the door for her. "Please tell my father that I'll be up in a few minutes, Abbey. I'm going to check the assembly line and see what has happened to our timetable."

Abbey nodded silently as he closed the door behind them and headed toward the assembly line. She leaned against the door and flexed her fingers, trying to get some movement back into her frozen muscles. The edges of the clipboard were imprinted in her palms. Now she recognized the feeling that had weakened her knees before. She was in trouble. She had fallen in love with Gabe Kendall! All these years she had waited to love a man, and the man she had found loved another woman. Ann Kendall was not the kind of competition that could be easily overcome. Abbey fought tears of mingled joy and pain. How could she ever compare with the beautiful memory of Ann?

Hoping to avoid people, Abbey climbed the back stairs. She needed solitude to collect her chaotic thoughts. Lesley had once described Ann Kendall as a "gracious lady." Abbey knew that she had been blond, blue-eyed and beautiful. Everyone who met Ann had loved her. All had admired her grace, tact and charm.

Tired, Abbey sat on the top step of the long stairwell. She wasn't quite up to the cheer on the second floor. She wished she had listened more to Amy when her friend had tried to give her advice on being "attractive to the opposite sex." Instead, she had laughed and believed in her heart that she couldn't love any man who preferred art and artifice to reality. Abbey was nothing if not real.

She looked down at the sturdy loafers on her feet and

thought that they characterized herself. Of course, high heels would be ridiculous on the dock, but they wouldn't have hidden the fact that she had well-shaped feet and ankles. Her tweed skirt and wool sweater kept her warm in her chilly office, but they would hardly make a man think of moonlight and roses. Still, Gabe had compared her to a rose the other night. He had said that some men liked roses better than orchids.

Abbey didn't let her hopes rise. Ann Kendall might have been a rose, too, but she was not one of the wild kind that grew up the side of a house. Ann had been an exotic tea rose to be cherished and used only in a centerpiece. Abbey felt drearily that if there was a rose like her, it was the state flower, the wild rose. It was a healthy pink bloom that covered old fences and barns in Iowa. Everyone loved it, but it was just taken for granted. No one made a fuss over a wild rose.

She realized how deeply she was falling into self-pity and shook her head with disgust. The Lord had not made her a great beauty, but He had not given her any great handicaps either. Some are made to be cared for, and some are made to do the caring, Abbey quoted an old saying of her mother's to herself. You bloom best where you are planted.

She stood up and smiled. She would not take anything but good news to Ralph, Ira and Lesley, who were waiting for her. She tucked her newfound knowledge deep in her heart. Ralph would enjoy knowing that his hired man had accidently brought along the family cat, who'd been sleeping in the truck. It had taken them half an hour to remove the feline from behind the front seat, so determined was it to go to Chicago. Ira would laugh at Amy driving her rental truck, while Lesley would giggle at the description of Gabe and his half-eaten sucker. She opened the door, her brown eyes shining. No one could take away from her the memory of that sweet kiss on the raw winter day.

Gabe headed across the work yard. His heart was singing in gratitude for the work done, for the town of Counsel and for Abbey Wilson. How could she have believed he would be angry with her for planning such a surprise? She had looked so frightened that he'd wanted to take her in his arms like a child and reassure her. Had she been upset by his kiss? He stopped dead. Had he offended her? She had almost melted into the brick wall at his approach. Had he become so terrifying to her? He thought of the night she had unpacked the dishes, when he must have seemed demented. He had apologized, hadn't he? He continued across the yard. Her hands had been so cold. He was going to buy her some fur-lined gloves. He stopped again. Was he completely mad? He couldn't go around buying gloves for a woman, an employee. The whole town would gossip. He would have Lesley buy them for Abbey. He was almost to the door when his foreman appeared with the cat, Solomon.

"Sir," said the foreman. "Your cat."

Gabe eyed Solomon with disfavor. "Oh yes, the stowaway."

"He howls," said the man succinctly. "In fact, he screams."

"What?"

"We locked him in a storeroom, but he tried to tear the door down. It upset the ladies on the line. They feel sorry for him, you know."

"Oh."

"We wondered if you might take him up to your office. It's dangerous over here with all of the machinery."

"Ah."

"Would you take him, Mr. Kendall, please?"

Gabe noticed that Solomon had all four paws deeply buried in the man's heavy down jacket. Gabe pulled the cat off and several feathers drifted from the tears in the coat. Gabe told the man to send the bill to him and, noticing the man's scratched hands, sent him to the nurse. There was nothing to do but haul the cat up to his office. When Solomon saw the door, he tried to climb up and over Gabe's head. Gabe grasped him firmly and went through the door, ignoring Solomon's bloodcurdling yowls all the way up the stairs. He was afraid to try the elevator for fear of his life.

Abbey had just come through the door after her thinking session on the stairs when Solomon's howling drew her attention to Gabe's predicament.

"Can you put him down?" she yelled helpfully over the din.

"Do you think I like carrying a cat imbedded in my scalp?" yelled Gabe back.

"Glory!" Abbey tried to soothe the upset animal, who was now wrapped tightly around Gabe's head and neck.

"Kindly remember," Gabe sputtered through the gray and white fur, "that he has the claws of his left paw above my jugular."

Gently, making crooning noises, Abbey coaxed Solomon down from his human perch. The event had now collected an interested audience consisting of Ralph, Ira, Lesley and various secretaries and clerks.

"What did you do to scare him like that?" barked Ralph,

taking the cat from Abbey's arms. "He's usually so docile."

"I narrowly saved my factory staff from being massacred. He scratched my foreman and slaughtered a down jacket in the process. Where did that cat come from?"

Ralph stroked the cat, who was curled up and purring on his lap. "He just wandered in one day and made friends."

Gabe looked at the crowd, who silently folded their tents, smothered their giggles and stole away.

Abbey appeared with a first-aid kit. "He's one of the Bailey kittens. They all have that half-white moustache. They're a tough breed of cat—wonderful hunters."

Gabe jumped as Abbey dabbed the score marks on his forehead. "Ouch! Dad should have called him Attila the Hun. I'm going to lock my door at night. He might carry me off to feed his friends."

Lesley lost all control at that point and whisked into Gabe's office with Ralph and Ira. Their laughter could be heard, slightly muffled, through the closed door.

Abbey pushed Gabe into Lesley's chair and continued to clean and apply antiseptic to the scratches. She smiled at Gabe. "It's just that it was a difficult morning and you and the cat gave everyone a chance to relax with a good laugh."

"Somehow I've never thought of myself as comic relief." Gabe looked up ruefully.

"It's the best medicine your father could have," Abbey commented.

Gabe sniffed appreciatively. "I like your perfume."

Abbey's hand froze during her ministrations. "Thank you. It's called Maytime."

"Smells like fresh-cut flowers."

Abbey sat on Lesley's desk to deal with the scratches on

Gabe's hand. "It's a shame you had to have this happen when everything else went so well. Field and farm cats are naturally frightened in the city."

"That cat wasn't frightened. He was mad because I stopped the bloodbath he had planned to execute in the cannery."

Abbey started to laugh. "Oh dear, I'm sorry, but it was funny. If only you could have seen yourself wearing that cat like a coonskin cap."

In the blandest of voices, Gabe addressed the wall behind her. "Animals used to like me. Employees used to take me seriously. My father used to care for me more than a vagabond cat. Obviously I'm losing my grip on reality."

Abbey tried to pull herself together, but couldn't look him in the eye. Instead, she resumed her first aid on his hand.

"Ouch!"

"You see, that should prove to you that you're real," she chortled.

"Thanks."

"You're welcome."

She finished and reluctantly released his hand, but he didn't move. His face was turned toward his office, where his father still chuckled with Ira and Lesley. "That's the first time I've heard my father laugh since Thanksgiving." He turned to her with warmth. "Thanksgiving was the first time he had laughed in two years."

Abbey nodded. "I know what you mean. I thought my father would starve to death after we lost Mom. He never remembered to eat or sleep. It was quite a while before he even smiled."

"I was wrong, Abbey. I thought he needed to be left

alone. But he's improved a hundred percent since Ira visited that day. You deserve an apology. I seem to have to do that a lot with you. Why is that?''

Abbey repacked the first-aid kit. ''My father says that you and I forget who is the parent. He feels that we shouldn't take decisions upon ourselves that are not ours to make. I don't think your father really wants to retire, and I know mine doesn't.''

Gabe grinned at the way she had avoided answering his question, but did not pursue the subject. He stood up and looked down at the gleaming chestnut hair. ''Thank you, anyway.''

He walked to the door of his office. She could hear the door open and the friendly teasing as his father joshed him about his ''battle wounds.'' She took the kit to her office and sat down at her desk still thinking about Gabe.

He had spoken of his father as though their grief were not shared. Abbey had wanted desperately to say, ''How long has it been since you felt good about yourself, Gabriel Kendall? What about medicine for what hurts you so? Give me a chance to wipe away those lines of pain as they disappeared today when you laughed at yourself.''

''Pull yourself together, Abbey Wilson,'' she said sternly. ''Even if he would let himself love again, it's not going to be good old pal Abbey he'll choose. You're not his type. A rose is a rose is a rose, and it is never going to be a gardenia! Get to work, or you're not even going to be an executive assistant.''

Abbey was involved in the mysteries of production charts when Lesley came and asked her to join them in Gabe's office. She grabbed and pad and pencil and followed Lesley, who stopped outside her office for a moment.

"You know, honey, it's just like the old days. Mr. Kendall is raring to go with new ideas." Lesley always spoke of Ralph as "Mr. Kendall" while using Gabe's first name. "Gabe is flashing back ideas as fast as Mr. Kendall throws them. Ira is egging them on. It's wonderful! The town helping like that just overwhelmed them. What a brilliant idea that was!" Lesley gave Abbey a motherly hug. "What a blessing it was when you interviewed for this job."

When Abbey arrived, a little pink-cheeked and flustered from the older woman's compliments, she was hailed by a chorus of men's voices.

Gabe let his father outline their plan to fete the town in honor of its accomplishment today. While Ralph talked, Gabe noticed how lovely Abbey looked in her green sweater that gave her dark brown eyes the depth of velvet. How gracefully the mahogany hair swept back from the sculptured line of her face. She had the deep, quiet beauty of a fine piece of porcelain or an Egyptian sculpture. She was not flashy or stunning like Amy. She was a prototype of woman that went back to Ruth, Naomi and Esther—ageless and arresting. He realized that everyone was looking to him for an answer to a question he hadn't heard.

"Back with us, son?" Ralph inquired. "Are your wounds bothering you?"

"Possible blood poisoning," said Gabe equably, glaring at the lump of sleeping fur in Ralph's lap. "I'm for a party. What kind would appeal to everyone?"

"We should have it catered so that no one would have to work," suggested Ralph.

Ira and Abbey were silent. The other three looked questioningly at them.

"Say it, Abbey," commanded Gabe. "I promise not to jump down your throat."

"Catering is a lovely idea, if you were going to have it here at the factory," Abbey said slowly.

"We're not going to have a party in the factory," roared Ralph.

"No one caters a meal here. I'm not sure people would be comfortable, especially the children. Although some would be unable to bring much to a party, they would want to contribute something."

"What kind of party is it that asks people to supply their own refreshments?" demanded Ralph.

"A Counsel party," chorused Ira and Abbey.

"I can't accept that," growled Ralph.

"Dad," interrupted Gabe, "accept it. I have found, to my sorrow, that it's not smart to ignore a Wilson's opinion. If you don't take their advice, you are inevitably going to be in the wrong."

Ralph looked at his son in utter confusion. "Have I heard correctly? Are you telling me that I should listen to someone else's advice other than yours?"

Gabe nodded.

"I never thought I'd see the day." Ralph's eyes twinkled.

Ira poked him in the ribs. "Listen and learn, old friend."

Gabe sat back and enjoyed watching his father experience the first injection into the mainstream of Counsel, Iowa, as administered by the Wilsons.

The rest of the week was spent getting ready for the Kendalls' party. Abbey and Lesley organized it as they had the church dinner. Since it was for the whole town, the whole town would be part of the preparations. That was the kind of party people could understand. Counsel enjoyed an event it was a part of. Its people didn't know how to sit back and be entertained; they were accustomed to being the party themselves.

Emma and the church circle prepared the house, putting away the fragile objects and moving furniture into patterns better suited to crowds. Large tables were borrowed to hold the food that would be brought by every household. The back parlor behind the living room had been cleared and prepared for the children. Mothers and teenagers would man the children's room in relays so that they could all enjoy the event, but everyone had a responsibility.

The theme was to be "A Happy Unbirthday to the Counsel Cannery." Abbey made the rounds from Millicent Shriers and her 4-H girls decorating cookies to Amy and her young women making chains of crepe paper and glue. Mama Scarpino was baking a cake in the shape of the cannery. Preparations went on in every household in and around Counsel.

The new truck line had shown up on time for the next load of soups, and Ross was happy and relaxed. Their schedule was humming along and the factory was torn between the fun of preparing for the party and the opening of the Christmas season.

Amy confided that the eight-hour conversation between herself and Ross on the way to Chicago had borne the fruit of friendship and more. Amy was fairly burbling in her enthusiasm for Ross Ellis. Abbey tried to see Ross through Amy's eyes as the "most handsome, most brilliant and most sensitive man in the world," but failed to see anything but Ross Ellis, a nice man and a good worker. She realized that it was Amy's love that made Ross a champion among men. She herself simply could not see how anyone could look at any other male when Gabriel Kendall was in the vicinity.

Abbey did all of her errands. She listened to everyone at work and at the church who needed her help or advice. She helped whoever asked her, but withdrew into herself.

Jordan Davis asked her to marry him for the umpteenth time, and she refused him. This time she begged him to stop for his sake and her own.

He looked at her sadly. "I guess you've just never felt that way about me, have you, Abbey? I'm real sorry. I've always loved you, you know."

Abbey felt deeply for his hurt, which she understood so well. What could be more painful than loving someone who didn't love you back? "I love you, Jordan. I've loved you like a brother all of my life. We've been friends all these years. Please, let's still be friends. I know you have a lot to give the woman you love—I just can't love you that way."

Jordan took her hand and kissed it. "I've always known. I just thought you might take me for want of someone better. I guess I thought I'd kinda wear you down just by being around. I know I'm not in the same class as Gabe Kendall. I can see how you feel about him: you feel about him the way I feel about you. I think you could make him happy, if anyone could, Abbey. I just don't think he will let anyone be that close again. I hope I'm wrong, for your sake. If you need a shoulder, give me a call."

Jordan went down the porch steps in calm dignity. He was such a dear man. Abbey felt a tremendous load of guilt. How could she explain to Jordan that she had not known how much it hurt until she was hurt herself? She went to bed that night and wept for Jordan, for Gabe and for herself.

"Please let me find a way to help him," she prayed. "Let him be happy, even if it's not with me. Give me the same kindness and generosity you gave to Jordan."

In honor of the party, Abbey took Ira to Des Moines and bought him a new suit to replace his shiny blue serge. They were enjoying a rest and cup of hot cocoa on a shopping center bench when Ira spotted the dress.

"Aha!" he said, dropping his empty cup into the wastebasket and grabbing Abbey. "That's for you."

The topaz velvet dress glimmered softly among the bright taffetas and red Christmas satins. Ira would not give up until Abbey had tried it on. The small puffed sleeves and snug waist outlined her trim figure until it swirled into the soft, circular skirt around her knees. It cost more than Abbey had ever spent on a dress in her life, but Ira insisted. Abbey loved the dress and hadn't the slightest desire to argue. After all, everyone would wear their best to the party. The amber velvet enhanced her creamy skin and put lights into her hair and eyes she had not seen before. She shook her head at her own extravagance as she watched the dress anxiously while the sales girl folded it into the tissue paper. Her mother had said to bloom where you were planted, but there was no reason not to bloom as prettily as possible.

Chapter Six

The old Johnson house was alive again. Abbey looked over from the receiving line to the crowd milling about the living room. Ladies were putting their covered dishes on the long tables in the dining room. The sound of children trilled from the little parlor. She greeted the Payne family, starting with Jo Ellen. Fred was pumping Gabe's hand next to her, while the two younger Paynes were being charmed by Ralph and Lesley at the head of the line.

Jo Ellen's apple-dumpling face was wreathed in smiles. "Isn't this fun? I told Fred I was going to break down and make my German cake for the occasion, even if it is only supposed to be for Christmas and birthdays! After all, this is a kind of birthday for Counsel, isn't it?"

Abbey heartily agreed with Jo Ellen and shook hands with Fred in turn before turning the family over to Ross and

Amy, who would lead them to the coatroom and take the culinary offerings.

Gabe was assuring Millicent that he couldn't wait to taste some of her pumpkin pie. Then it was Abbey's turn to be hugged and enveloped in a cloud of cinnamon and spice.

"You are gorgeous tonight, my dear," Millicent whispered in her ear. "That dress is the cat's pajamas."

"It cost more than the cat," Abbey whispered back.

"Lilies deserve a little gilding," Millicent said out loud. She turned to give her coat to Amy and handed her pie to Ross. Laughing, they exchanged the items and escorted Millicent into the crowd.

Jordan came through the line with Susan Martin, the school librarian from the next town. Abbey was pleased to see him dating someone else. He looked at her sorrowfully as he took in her new dress, but only made the smallest of conversation.

Susan said softly to Abbey, "You aren't mad, are you?" Her face was anxious.

Abbey hugged her and assured her that Jordan was a dear friend, but more of a brother than a boyfriend. "I think you'd be great for each other, Susie. That blue dress really compliments your eyes. You have a good time tonight!"

Susan smiled and her face lit up with happiness. Abbey thought that Jordan could do a lot worse than fall in love with kind-hearted Susie, who was popular with everyone.

At last most of the guests seemed to have arrived. Amy handed the four from the receiving line their red punch. Gabe took an appreciative sip.

"Ah, Emma Davis's red cider!"

Abbey sipped her cider and admired Gabe while Lesley and Ralph discussed the possibilities of making the red cider a product for next year. Gabe was watching the crowd, so that she could feast her eyes on him unobserved. He was impressive in a midnight-blue suit that was specially cut to accommodate his wide shoulders and narrow waist. The blue of his shirt was an exact match for his eyes. Abbey drank in all of the details to savor later. She would go over each tidbit in her mind and enjoy them at leisure: how small the punch cup looked in his hand, how clear his eyes were, how much younger he looked when he smiled.

Ira touched her elbow, and she turned to see her father regarding her with troubled eyes. "I'm sorry, Dad. Just daydreaming, I guess."

Ira didn't have to ask her what the subject was. He had seen that same look in her mother's eyes when they were young together. He sent up a quick prayer that her hopes would not be in vain.

"We have a small program," Ira announced. "If Ralph and Gabe will follow me, please." He led them to a place in front of the fireplace in the living room.

Emma Davis took the floor first and announced that, thanks to Ralph and Gabe Kendall, the temporary public library that was now housed in the church basement would in the future be permanently established in the old store next to the Payne Grocery Store. The Counsel Town Library would be gifted by a trust set up by the Kendalls for the purpose of paying overhead and buying new books.

The foreman of the factory stepped forward with a cloth-wrapped object in his hand. "The folks in the factory would like to show their appreciation to Mr. Gabe Kendall." He turned to Gabe. "This is to thank you for courage in the face of adversity and bravery beyond the call of duty." With that he pulled off the cloth to reveal a trophy. It was in the shape of a large cat sitting with one paw lifted. Everyone had heard the story of Solomon and Gabe by now. There wasn't a sound in the room except for small children playing in the parlor.

Abbey held her breath. If only she could tell Gabe that the town had extended their highest compliment to him as a person: they had shared a joke with him. Slowly Gabe took the trophy and read the inscription aloud.

"Courage in the face of adversity and bravery beyond the call of duty." He turned to look at the audience. With a straight face he studied the award. "I am happy to accept this trophy in the spirit in which it is given. As the recipient of the first Savage Solomon Award, let me assure you that it will be cherished with a deep sense of humility—and terror. I feel that Solomon himself should share this moment. If you will wait a minute, I will let him out of the basement to accept in person."

"Oh no!" exclaimed the foreman.

"No!" shouted the crowd with one voice.

Gabe threw back his head and roared with laughter, to be joined by everyone.

"Oh good," exulted Abbey quietly. "Good for Gabe!"

Gabe set the trophy in the middle of the mantel and, taking out his handkerchief, polished its base.

The next gift was for Ralph from the ladies of Counsel. It was a quilt with each square representing an aspect of the town. Emma Davis told everyone that it had been originally designed as a Christmas present for the Kendalls, but the ladies had hurried to finish it in time for the party.

Amy told Abbey that she had embroidered the square representing the bank. "I felt it would please my father to see I could do something fairly well. Did you see Milli-cent's square? She designed and stitched the cannery, complete with gargoyles!''

Each woman wanted to show Abbey which square was their work. She admired everyone's, especially Emma's square, representing the church. All of the landmarks, businesses and farms were represented on the king-sized quilt.

"It took thirty of us to hand-quilt it," Jo Ellen said with satisfaction. "It should last a generation or two."

Abbey patted the soft cotton and praised everyone for their hard work. The quilt was displayed over the back of a long sofa. It represented Counsel at its best—a gift of imagination that would be appreciated for years to come.

Three of the Baileys were ushered out of the kitchen. They had eaten early so that they could provide music for the rest of the group. A space was soon cleared around the piano for the pianist, the fiddler and the banjo player. Music was the Baileys' gift to the party, and Mrs. Bailey's square on the quilt was a banjo crossed by a fiddle.

The crowd surged behind Lesley and the Kendalls to the tables. It took hours to serve everyone because of the coming and going of various families. More dishes arrived and were decimated, kids consumed gallons of milk and Abbey refilled the coffee maker countless times. Above all, the famous red cider continued to flow.

Mama Scarpino's cannery cake disappeared in minutes, to be replaced by a succession of homemade cakes that represented the favorite recipe of each family.

Abbey laughed and worked with each group of servers throughout the evening. She thanked the 4-H girls, who were washing the punch cups and dishes as fast as people could empty them. She complimented each woman on her offering. She made sure the new families had someone to talk to. She kept the older men happy with trays of cider and gentle teasing.

Although she'd caught Amy's smile from across the room, she had little time to talk with her friend. People came in waves and spilled into the hallways and rooms of the big old farmhouse. She saw Gabe swimming through crowds of people, shaking hands and laughing. Ira was always surrounded. The shouts of the children wound in and out of the adult cheer like a bright ribbon. An elated Abbey knew that she had a successful party on her hands.

Lesley passed by with her pink cheeks reflecting the color of her lovely rose silk gown. They smiled at each other on their ways to different areas with trays of cookies and punch. Abbey refilled Ralph's cup, since he was trapped by a bevy of charming matrons. So many hands reached out to her below happy faces that the room became a carrousel of compliments and chatter. She loved it.

Gabe happened to see Abbey as she was rescuing a toddler from underneath the big oak table. The little boy threw his arms around her neck as she held him to her. His small round head was nestled against her shoulder, and she momentarily rested her cheek on the dark curls. Gabe's breath caught at the age-old beauty of the scene. Then the child's mother smilingly retrieved her child and Abbey turned to help someone else. Gabe felt distinctly guilty. He had not meant for her to have the full burden of organizing the party. He thought it would just carry itself along by momentum. He realized how simplistic that idea had been after the third group of people had come and gone. It seemed to him that she had introduced him to hundreds of people, and all by name. Did she know everyone? Everyone seemed to know her. She was always surrounded by a whirlpool of bodies. He hadn't even had a chance to tell her how pretty she looked in the soft gold dress. A remark in his direction submerged him into the party and he lost sight of Abbey once more.

Around eleven the last group of revelers began to move toward the door. Emma and Zeb Davis had sensibly taken the last shift and were putting away perishables and washing up the last dishes as Abbey and Lesley ferreted cups and plates out from under chairs. The teenagers had cleared the parlor of children's litter. A cleanup crew was coming in the next day to set things to rights and move back the furniture.

At the end there was only a small group left. Ralph handed cups to Ira, who washed them while Lesley dried, Gabe stacked and Abbey and Amy put them in boxes. Ross carried the cups out to his car to take back to the rental shop in the morning.

Emma and company left, so that Ralph, Ira, Lesley, Amy, Ross, Gabe and Abbey could collapse in the living room.

"You should be in bed," Gabe advised his father.

"Try putting me there and I'll run you over in this chair," threatened Ralph. "The best part of a party is the postmortem."

"He fired his nurse," Gabe informed the others.

"I don't need a nurse," growled Ralph.

"I may, after this party," moaned Gabe. "I must have eaten forty different kinds of cakes and pies."

"Everyone wanted you to taste their specialty," Abbey explained.

"Besides, you worked it all off," added Ross. "I must have walked ten miles tonight running the ladies' errands."

"You wouldn't want us to carry all of those heavy trays," purred Amy.

"If you are the weaker sex, why are you all looking fresh and all the men looking frazzled?" Ross retorted.

"Speak for yourself, Ross," said Ralph. "I feel great!"

"It was a nice party," Ira contributed.

"Such delightful people," Lesley agreed.

Abbey was enjoying the euphoric feeling that all good hostesses feel when their party has gone well. Ira looked handsome in his new suit with his hair slightly ruffled. Lesley was as unruffled and perky as ever. Ross relaxed next to Amy in his rakish, loose-jointed sprawl while Amy looked regal in her vanilla dull-satin dress. Ralph's eyes were still sparkling, and Gabe, as always, was Gabe. She felt positively triumphant.

"It was a wonderful party."

They all agreed. Each had an anecdote to share with the others. They discussed the guests' remarks and their reactions. Gabe laughed about the trophy and said he was going to dip the lifted paw in red paint so that it would be realistic. Suddenly it was midnight and Gabe insisted that his father get some sleep. Ralph was hauled off complaining bitterly.

At the door, Gabe asked over his shoulder if Ross would go with him to the factory. "I saved some of the treats for the night watchman. I thought you might go with me to take them over to him."

Ross eyed Gabe with dismay as he wheeled his father out.

He had promised to take Amy home. Emil had already left. The disappointment was evident in his crestfallen expression.

Amy said bravely, "I can go home with Abbey."

Abbey took pity on them. "Go ahead and take Amy home, Ross. I'll go with Gabe. He can drop me off on the way home from the factory."

Ira raised an eyebrow but said nothing. He assisted Lesley into her coat, as he had offered her a ride home. He thought a moment and said, "Perhaps we could all go with Gabe."

Lesley grabbed his arm so tightly that he was startled. "Let the young people go," she said. "I'm tired, aren't you? Old Mr. Petty will enjoy having a young lady bring him treats." Lesley practically dragged Ira to the door.

"Maybe I'd better stay," Ross said, worried.

"No," said Amy definitely. Her eyes met with Lesley's. "I haven't had a chance to talk with you alone since the ride to Chicago. Lesley's right. Mr. Petty will love seeing Abbey in her party dress."

Ira and Ross had the feeling that they were being pushed rather quickly out the doors to their cars, but the company was so enchanting that they let themselves be pulled along.

Gabe came down the stairs to find Abbey waiting for him. He looked surprised.

"Ross had to take Amy home," Abbey explained. "I'm standing in for him, if that's all right. We've kept them so busy this week that they have hardly had a moment to themselves."

"I see. Of course, a pretty girl will be more fun for Mr. Petty. It also gives me a chance to thank you for all you've done. You did a great job with the party. My father was still saying that he was glad he listened to your ideas. I can see where a catered affair would have fallen flat.''

''Oh no,'' Abbey hastened to reassure him. ''Everyone would have tried very hard to respond to whatever you would have done for them. It's just that, in a small town, people like to be part of everything. They're used to taking care of themselves. They would have tried to please you, no matter what.''

''Because of the cannery?''

''You saved the town, Mr. Kendall.''

''I thought you were going to call me Gabe.''

''We owe you a lot, but that didn't make the party successful. If they hadn't personally liked you, they would have been merely polite.''

''Wasn't it because of you and Ira?''

''I don't understand.''

''It seemed to me that it was you, Ira and Amy who made the party work.''

''The trophy was for you,'' Abbey reminded him.

''I enjoyed that.'' He smiled. ''No one ever did anything like that in Chicago. There was so much distance between the men and women who worked in the factory and management.''

''Yes.''

''Did I tell you how lovely your dress is?''

Abbey looked startled at the change of subject. She sensed that he wanted her to say that the town really liked him. He needed to feel that he was more than just an employer. It was difficult to speak when what she really wanted to do was to put her arms around this man and hold him and comfort him. She wanted to tell him that she loved him. She longed to tell him that the town cared about him and his father as friends, not just bosses. She wished to smooth out that line between his brows with loving fingers and kiss that firm mouth.

Gabe saw her eyes darken and found himself noticing how full and tender her mouth was against her translucent skin. The amber dress seemed to shimmer around her, and he was drawn to put his hand against the vulnerable column of her slender throat. She was so beautiful.

Abbey lifted her arms up to his shoulders to draw him down toward her. Her dream was going to come true after all. She closed her eyes as he bent down to kiss her.

"Gabe!" Ralph's voice shouted from upstairs. "You can let Solomon out of the basement now. He always sleeps on my bed."

Gabe straightened up. His eyes were a very dark blue. "Right." His mouth quirked up on one side and Abbey laughed at his expression rather shakily. "Let the cat out of the basement." He went away muttering about cats under his breath to reappear followed by a ruffled Solomon.

Gabe and Abbey watched the cat glare balefully at them before he turned and stalked up the stairs bearing his tail like a royal train.

"That," said Gabe, "is precisely why my father named him King Solomon." He looked down at Abbey with humor. "We'd best deliver Mr. Petty's goodies to him before he gives up all hope."

Abbey's heart plummeted. It was as though he had just turned off his feelings. He went to get the basket for the night watchman as she found her coat and shrugged herself into it. Should she speak to him? Didn't she give him enough encouragement? Had he somehow felt that she wasn't willing? What had she done that put him off? Obviously the romantic moment had been interrupted by Ralph, but was it so difficult to recapture? Bewildered, Abbey followed Gabe out of the house to the car.

They drove in silence to the cannery and located Mr. Petty, who was overcome by their thoughtfulness. It was a long time before they could tear themselves away from his enthusiastic gratitude. Abbey was grateful to Mr. Petty for breaking the ice between her and Gabe. There was a much friendlier atmosphere in the car on the way to the parsonage. Ira's old car was in the driveway. Only the kitchen light was on, indicating he had gone to bed. Gabe stopped the car and stared ahead through the windshield in silence. Abbey wondered if she should get out and leave him to his thoughts, or wait until he felt like sharing them. She shivered.

One long arm reached out and gathered her to him. He captured her hands in one of his. "I seem to be responsible for your hands being cold a good deal of the time." She let her head rest against his shoulder and prayed for no interruptions, content just to be near him. "You are strangely silent, miss, for a lady who usually has so much to say."

Wisely, Abbey kept silent and turned so that her cheek rested on his chest. She was delighted to note that his heart was beating faster than normal. He kissed her soft, fragrant hair and buried his face in it. Abbey let herself rest against him, making no demands—simply enjoying his closeness. He released her hands so that he could tip her face up to his.

He let his lips brush her forehead, cheeks and eyes until she slid her arm around his neck and raised her lips to his. The warmth of his mouth called up an answering heat from hers. She drowned in that kiss given to him with all of her heart. When he released her, she was not shivering from the cold.

"In," he commanded gruffly, releasing her. He took her hand and pulled her out of the car.

"Would you like some cocoa?" she asked hopefully.

"Do you like to live dangerously?" Gabe rasped. He opened the door and almost pushed her into the kitchen. Abbey turned to say good night, but he was already halfway to the car.

Sheba meowed at the door and Abbey let her in. "Where have you been? No, don't tell me. I know that look." The cat rubbed up against her ankles. "That's what I thought."

Abbey turned off the kitchen lights and climbed the stairs slowly, mulling over her time spent with Gabe. It had been an eventful night, if a confusing one. She had no idea of what to do. She felt like one of the TV heroines of the early fifties who looked into the camera in amazement saying, "Who was that masked man?"

Gabe had alternately raised her to the heights and dropped her to the lower depths in a few short hours. She had received what she had hoped for, but she still did not know Gabe Kendall any better than before. The banked fires in his kiss convinced her that he was attracted to her, but his hasty exit left her wondering. Sighing, she hung the velvet dress in her old armoire. The whole evening had been like skiing on mountaintops—you were never quite sure where the drop-off would appear.

Four months ago she had believed that Gabe would never

smile, let alone laugh. Now he was participating in town parties and jokes. Had his kiss been one of simple gratitude for the party? No. Abbey couldn't believe that. That kind of kiss had a great deal more behind it than mere appreciation of a job well done. She just couldn't get behind the mask to the man. The layers peeled away, but Abbey never got to the core of the man.

Abbey's heart froze with a new thought. Did he pretend it was not her he was kissing, but someone else? Were his eyes closed, not in passion, but in order to pretend that he had Ann back in his arms again?

Abbey hugged her pillow in anguish. She knew she could never believe in Gabe's love until she was sure that it was her he loved. Then she caught herself and shook her emotions awake. "One kiss does not a lifetime make, dummy. You're building mountains out of molehills again. Be practical. Be sensible. Like Dad said—let the Lord handle it."

She looked up with hope. She knew the Lord would handle it, but was there any way she could help things along?

The next day Abbey met at the Kendall house with Amy, Lesley and the cleanup crew. The men pushed back the furniture while the ladies vacuumed and packed decorations and dishes.

Jordan took a garbage sack of crepe paper from Abbey. "You sure looked pretty last night."

"I thought Susie Martin looked awfully good," Abbey said with a grin.

Jordan grinned back. "She likes me."

Abbey tied the sack shut and looked him squarely in the

eye. "Susie is a lovely person, Jordan. We've always been friends. Her blue eyes are as pretty as your mom's, you know."

"They are pretty," Jordan agreed. "We're going to a movie in Ames tonight."

Abbey kissed him on the cheek. "You have a good time."

"You're sure?" Jordan hedged. "This may be your last chance at me, Abbey."

Abbey suppressed a smile at his seriousness. "I'm sure, Jordan. Friends?"

"Friends." He gave her a brotherly kiss. "Always."

Gabe's voice cut into their conversation. "If that's stuff to burn, we're ready for it."

As Gabe and Jordan headed toward the kitchen door, Gabe avoided looking at Abbey even once. Her shoulders slumped slightly—he could have said a simple hello. Amy nudged her friend sleepily. Amy hated to rise after a party until afternoon—late afternoon.

"If you want a man to like you, you shouldn't kiss other men in his presence."

Abbey shook her head in disbelief. "Jordan?"

"Jordan is a man." Amy yawned.

"But he's like a brother," argued Abbey.

"Maybe I'm not the one you should be telling that to."

"That's silly."

"Uh-huh, you didn't see Gabe Kendall's face. I did."

Lesley bustled by and handed them some boxes to store, which ended the conversation, but Abbey wished she *had* seen the expression on Gabe's face. She shrugged the idea away. Amy was a romantic.

Abbey decided that she wouldn't push herself at Gabe. If he didn't want to notice her today, that was his privilege. She worked with everyone else and left when the others left. She waved at Ralph sitting on the porch and got into Ira's car with Amy and Lesley. Ira had a wedding rehearsal that afternoon and wouldn't be home for supper, so she accepted Lesley's offer of coffee, as did Amy.

Lesley's little house was as compact and charming as the lady herself. Abbey and Amy were impressed by the cream walls, cherrywood furniture and lacy curtains, all feminine without being cloying. They sat around Lesley's kitchen table and looked out at her little garden.

"Wait until spring." Lesley put a plate of cookies in the middle of the table. "I'm going to grow every vegetable that will grow out there. I'm going to can and store and indulge in all of my nesting instincts."

"How long did you live in Chicago?" Amy lazily stirred her coffee.

"I was Mr. Kendall's secretary for over twenty years before Gabe took over. Gabe's secretary didn't want to relocate, so he brought me along. Mr. Kendall knew I'd come from a small town. I was like you, Abbey. I had come from a little town in Kansas, but I went to Chicago. I met and married my husband, Ed, there. He died eight years ago. I just kept on working. I wanted to retire to a little town again, and this seemed like a good chance, especially now that things are looking better."

Abbey looked questioningly at the older woman. "Better?"

Lesley stared down at her hands. "It was breaking my

heart to see the Kendalls suffer. You didn't notice it so much in Chicago because of Mr. Kendall's stroke and Gabe's coming and going. I didn't realize how much Gabe had changed until we arrived in Counsel. There's more time to notice things here.''

"Like what?" Amy asked bluntly.

Lesley hesitated. "You've done so much for them, Abbey. Amy is going to hear it from Ross anyway. Ralph Kendall's stroke didn't come from a reaction to the accident. It came because of Gabe. That's why Gabe gave up everything and moved to Counsel for his father. It happened when they were making arrangements for the funeral. You know, Abbey, that your father and Mr. Kendall were in the seminary together. When the family was killed, Mr. Kendall found great solace in his faith. He was talking with his pastor about the arrangements when Gabe arrived in a fury. He said he wasn't going to have his family buried from a church. He was out of his mind with grief, of course, but he refused to let them be buried in their faith. His father was terribly upset and argued with him. Gabe said that a just God would never have killed innocent people; therefore, there was no God. He raved at them both, his father and the pastor. I know, I was there helping with the arrangements and keeping lists. Gabe's face was a frightening sight. Believe me, I was terrified. The pastor started to quote some passage of Scripture, I can't even remember what it was. Gabe drew back his arm to strike the man and his father struggled with him. That's when he had his stroke!"

Abbey took Lesley's hands in hers. The woman was trembling in agitation.

"To please his father, Gabe let them be buried from the church, but he just sat through the ceremony like a dead man. I never saw him weep one tear for any of them: his mother, his brother, his wife or children. It was like something died inside him. Abbey, you don't realize how much you've done. I prayed he would meet someone like you, someone who could bring him back to life."

"Wait a minute, Lesley." Amy frowned. "I'm glad Abbey has helped, but I'm not sure she needs to take on the salvation of Gabe Kendall."

"Amy!" Abbey shot a reproving look at her friend.

"What if he's too far gone, Abbey?" Amy said quietly. "You have a life of your own to live. You've always given your life away to others. It's not fair to make this man a lifetime project. He may not ever be able to get beyond pleasant conversation and an occasional smile. I know you—you never give up. He may be dead inside. I don't want you to fall in love with a man who can never give you anything back. When is your time coming, Abbey? You deserve to be loved completely by a man. This man may never be whole again."

"It's too late, Amy." Abbey was saddened by the glisten of tears in Amy's eyes.

"That's what I was afraid of," Amy groaned.

Lesley looked ashamed. "Amy may be right, Abbey. I have been loyal to the Kendalls for all these years, and I do always think of them first. Gabe is like a son to me, for the Lord never sent us children. I made Gabe and his brother, Michael, my adopted children." She rose heavily from her chair and looked out the window into the dreary winter sky.

"Amy's your friend; she's thinking of you. Ira spoke to me last night. He worries, too. He saw Amy and me help get you two together after the party. He feels that Gabe should be healed first before attempting a new relationship."

"How do you heal without loving?" asked Abbey simply.

Chapter Seven

"There's no nail up here!" Amy crawled down from the ladder and shook a mittened finger at Abbey. "Some of the nails have fallen out!"

"I'll put one in and check the others." Abbey started up the ladder, carrying the hammer. "You check the rest of the bulbs and see if they're all working."

"Why didn't you do this before the cold hit?" lamented Amy.

"I usually do, but the party and my job put it out of my mind this year." Abbey hammered the nail in crookedly and pulled it out again. "Then I had to help Dad get the chess trip organized, and that took more time." The nail was still crooked, so she gave it a whack that bent it up toward the roof. "I promised Dad that the lights and the stable would be up before they got back Saturday night."

Abbey slithered down the ladder. She wasn't terribly fond of heights.

"That ladder must date back to the town's founding," Amy grumbled.

With an encouraging smile, Abbey handed her friend another string of lights and watched her crawl up the ladder. Fortunately Amy had a good head for heights. It was getting dark, and Abbey wanted to finish outlining the eaves of the parsonage. At least they could finish the front porch using the porch light.

It had been a hectic day. She had waved Ira, Ralph and the men's Chess Club off right after work. They were a little late and eager to be off to the tournament in Des Moines. The matches started around eight Friday morning. Ira had only gone with Abbey's promise that the Christmas decorations and nativity scene would be in place by the weekend.

"Abbey," shouted Amy, "this plug won't fit into the socket!" Amy trudged down the ladder once more. She turned to face Abbey and caught a faceful of snow. Another snowball hit Abbey from behind. Amy wiped her eyes and glared over Abbey's shoulder.

"Ross! You sneak! I wasn't ready for that."

Amy and Abbey scooped up snow and attacked the hapless Ross unmercifully. Amy was sitting on his chest and washing his face with snow when ammunition from another source warned them that someone else had joined the fray. The ladies were caught in the same kind of crossfire that had trapped Ross.

"Aha!" yelped Ross happily, scenting victory. "Gabe was a pitcher for his baseball team." He dived after Amy and brought her down into a snowdrift. "I was on the swim team."

Abbey ducked behind a bush as a volley of snowballs flew through the air. She waved her white mitten in the air. "Truce! Truce! We surrender!"

"That wasn't much of a battle." Two mischievous blue eyes peered at her over the barrier. Gabe extended a hand to untangle her from the bushes. There was much giggling and mirth coming from the direction of Amy and Ross's snowdrift. "You've lost a mitten." He retrieved the article and handed it to her.

"It was more of an ambush." Abbey grinned. "You don't have any snow on you."

"Of course not," Gabe answered with a distinct lack of modesty.

"Oh well." Abbey nonchalantly pushed him over the bushes into the snow.

"Foul!" Gabe sputtered from behind the shrubs as Abbey ran for cover.

A few minutes later, looking like abominable snow-women, Abbey and Amy yelled "uncle" in chorus, much to the satisfaction of the white-covered male figures beside them. All four sat panting on the front porch steps.

"Oh no! It's nearly dark!" Abbey jumped to her feet and looked sternly at the other three. "I promised Dad those lights would be up."

Meekly Gabe and Ross took the hammer, nails and flashlight. Gabe began climbing the ladder. Abbey's heart rejoiced. She had spent days in misery because of him. After the party he had returned to his perfect employer role, only speaking to her when necessary. He had even delivered tasks and lists via Lesley so that he and Abbey would not be alone.

Ross was shouting directions to the dim figure at the top of the ladder and being generally hilarious. "We're starving." He tried unsuccessfully to look pathetic. "We were on our way to Mama's for food when we saw you two damsels in distress. How do you like our style of rescue?"

"It's a little strenuous," commented Amy, "but effective."

After the eaves were strung and the porch was outlined, Abbey flipped the switch. The old house shone in the colored lights like the gingerbread house in the magic forest. They put away the tools and all marched off to Mama's for hot food.

Over dessert Abbey happened to mention ingenuously that if someone had a car, it would be nice to pick up the Christmas tree that the Paynes were holding for her.

The "someone" with the car offered to help with chivalrous good humor. Getting the tree turned out to be quite interesting. Since Gabe didn't have a rope in his car, the tree rested on the roof by dint of Ross sitting in one open window, holding on to it, while Gabe sat on the opposite side. Abbey cautiously drove the sedan down the slippery street while beside her Amy laughed herself into a fit of minor hysterics.

It took the men almost two hours to set the tree up in its stand by the front window. The trunk had to be sawed off because it hadn't been cut evenly. The tree was then discovered to have a crooked trunk. Much to Gabe's disgust, Ross was so weak from laughter that he was unable to hold it straight. Abbey and Amy fortified the troops with coffee, cake and jovial comments. At last the tree stood alone. Glaring at the Scotch pine with animosity, Gabe collapsed into an old armchair.

"Move, and I'll saw you into kindling," he threatened the tree as he took a cup of coffee from Abbey. "What is that tree made of? Iron?"

"Smells good." Amy sniffed the air.

"It's probably wounded in a hundred places," commented Abbey.

"Tough," said Gabe and Ross together.

Abbey slid into her favorite rocking chair. "Tomorrow Amy and I are repainting the nativity figures to be set up on Saturday. Then the Christmas season will officially begin."

"Tomorrow?" Amy and Ross looked at each other with dismay.

"Oh, Abbey! I didn't realize." Amy threw Ross a conciliatory glance. "Well, we'll just skip the play."

"I've had the tickets for two weeks." Ross tried not to sound disgruntled.

"Don't change your plans," begged Abbey. "It's nothing, really. You told me about going to that musical at the Civic Center, Amy. We both forgot."

"Are you saying that an evening with me is not a memorable experience?" Ross quipped.

"The party pushed a lot of things into the background." Amy looked at Gabe accusingly. "We all lost track of time."

"That is my cue to say I would be glad to help paint," Gabe sighed with resignation.

"Hey, that's very nice of you," said Ross with an evil grin. "I know Abbey will accept your kind offer, won't you, Abbey?"

"It's not that big a deal." Abbey had no desire to force Gabe to help her, nor did she want to spoil Ross and Amy's date. "I was only letting Amy come for the company. It's just a touch-up job."

"She did say the sheep were flaking." Amy looked up guiltily.

"Couldn't we do it now?" asked Ross.

Abbey looked at the clock. "It's too late. We have to work tomorrow."

Gabe stood and fixed everyone with a gimlet eye. "Now hear this. We will all go home to get some sleep. Tomorrow night I will take Amy's place as official paint assistant while Amy and Ross fulfill their plans. That's an order!"

Abbey, Amy and Ross saluted. "Yes, sir!"

"Hey," Amy remarked, "I don't work for him!"

Ross grabbed his coat and hustled Amy into hers. "He doesn't know that. He thinks everyone works for him."

Amy called over Ross's shoulder, "Do I get a salary?"

Ross pushed her out the door. "Do you want to get fired?"

Gabe followed them in mock severity. "Forward, march! On the double!" Abbey curtsied and handed him his hat. He took it and gently touched her cheek. "See you tomorrow. Charge!" Abbey watched him help Ross and Amy into the car and drive off. The night that had been so filled with joy was suddenly quiet. She let Neb in to sniff suspiciously around the tree. They'd put him out because he had an unfortunate habit of trying to sit in people's laps. Sheba was still sleeping on top of the corner cupboard in the living room.

Abbey turned off all the lights and headed up the stairs. She paused at the landing to look out the oval window. One bright star shone in the sky, dimming the luminescence of the others. "So he is to me," Abbey thought. "In a million men he would shine the brightest. The waiting was worth it, even if he is too far away for me to touch. I am not stupid enough to believe that I have touched him or known him yet." She continued on to her room. One word ran through her mind over and over: tomorrow. . . .

"Would it hurt if this sheep is cross-eyed?" Gabe studied the figure with alarm. "My brush slipped."

Abbey took her paint rag and wiped the offending eye. "It would bother the children to have a cross-eyed lamb in the stable. The paper would get at least five letters on the subject. Believe me."

Gabe dabbed paint on the spot again. "There. Now he has perfect twenty-twenty vision."

Abbey put the last bit of gold on one of the Wise Men's box of frankincense and sat back on her heels. "That's it."

Gabe unfolded his long legs and stuck his brush in a jar of turpentine. "I had no idea this project would include two cows, two donkeys and an entire herd of sheep."

"When I was little, there were only two sheep. The kids decided that the shepherds needed a herd. We raised the money ourselves."

"I like the little black sheep best."

"He was my idea. I named him Prodigal. I always loved him best because he was different."

"Is that why you've helped my father and me so much? Because we're the black sheep of the town? The different ones?"

Abbey was stunned by the question. Was that how he saw her? Was she just a do-gooder in his eyes? She considered her answer. "The whole town helped you, not just me. Your father and mine are old friends. It was natural that you would be made welcome. I haven't done anything more than anyone else."

"I don't believe that."

"Please do. I'm speaking of the cannery, the party and normal social courtesy." She took a deep breath. "I must admit that kissing you was my own idea entirely. I did that purely from selfish motives. I wanted to kiss you."

Gabe blinked at her honesty. He hadn't expected her to mention anything personal. Abbey could almost hear his mind switch gears. She wished she were a more diplomatic person. Certainly Amy could have handled this situation with more aplomb. Why did she have this dreadful habit of blurting out truths at the worst possible moment? She tried to hide her embarrassment by furiously cleaning her brushes.

The silence in the church basement echoed in her ears. She nearly decapitated one brush in her agitation. She could hear the papers that protected the floor rustle as he rose. "That's it," she mourned to herself. "I've offended his male sensibilities."

His long body eased down beside hers. "Abbey." Gentle fingers removed the brush from her hand.

She sat there, staring at her empty hands.

"Abbey." He touched her cheek, brushing back tendrils of dark hair. "We have to talk."

"I thought we were," she murmured.

"About us."

"Oh."

"Has it occurred to you that you have no future with me?"

Abbey met his eyes squarely. "No, it hasn't."

He took one of her paint-stained hands in his, rubbing his thumb over her palm delicately. She sat there immobile, hypnotized by the soothing motion that sent flames of pleasure up her arm. "It must be obvious to you that I enjoy your company."

She took a deep breath. "Sometimes it is. Sometimes it isn't."

"You make me laugh."

"That's me. They call me Abbey, the resident Counsel comic."

"Stop that. You know what I mean. If it weren't for you, we Kendalls would have a very different relationship with Counsel. You and your father have made us feel at home here. I know you were behind the town transportation day. They did that for you."

"Please don't make me out a saint." Abbey's hand closed around his. "Counsel owes you a lot. They were happy to help. After all, you are their angel. Without your backing the cannery, the town might have died. Please don't say you like me only because of those small favors. That demeans both of us."

"Abbey, I can't lie to you. I won't lie to you. You're dear and sweet and deserve the best life has to offer. You should have bright beginnings. All I have to offer is endings. I'm only here because of my father. I felt I owed him his wishes about retirement. If it weren't for Dad, I wouldn't be here."

Abbey took his hand in both of hers. "Where would you be, Gabe?"

"I honestly don't know. I assume you know about the accident."

"Yes. Lesley told me so that I could understand."

"Then you must understand that most of me died in that crash along with my family. The only thing that kept me going was the debt I owed to my father. I lived in a kind of fog. The work was easy to do. I just kept signing papers and dealing with reports, graphs and presentations. Nothing threatened my existence, because I had stopped existing. Grief is a kind of natural anesthetic. Dad had his faith, and that seemed to help him. I had nothing."

Abbey's fingers tightened around his hand, but she held her tongue and did not voice the heartache she felt at his words. Anything she could say at this moment would sound like preaching. A listener was what he needed now.

"I could feel a crack in the iceberg when I saw all of those trucks, campers and family cars lined up to take the soup to Chicago. I'd already felt small fissures opening up when we went to your house for Thanksgiving. I wanted to give more, but I had to run away from all of you because I know that loving becomes agony when you lose it. The only safe way to live is not to give hostages to fortune. No one can hurt you if you don't love. Abbey, I don't want to get involved with anyone again. I can't love anyone again. All I could offer you would be a kind of affection for the generous person you are. That can't be enough to make you happy."

Abbey turned around to face him directly. "You may not have faith in yourself, but I have faith in you, Gabe Kendall. I won't ask for what you cannot give. But I believe that you have more to give than you know."

"Abbey," he interrupted.

"Half a loaf is better than none. Millicent Shriers taught us that when she taught us to bake. It's a good saying."

"You should marry that young man who hangs around you, the Davis fellow. You would be happy on a farm with a flock of kids." Gabe helped Abbey up and released her. "He obviously cares about you."

Abbey was exasperated. "Jordan is a dear, big brother. He's now going out with a good friend of mine, Susan Martin."

"He didn't look at you like a brother."

"Susan is much better for Jordan than I," Abbey stated firmly. "She will fit into his needs in a way I never could. He doesn't know that yet, but Susie does. She is perfect for him."

"Do you make a habit of being a matchmaker?" inquired Gabe as he rolled up a sheet of newspaper covered with paint. "You are encouraging Ross and Amy, I believe. Not only that, I think Lesley has taken a liking toward your father."

Abbey looked up with a smile. "Do you think so? That would be wonderful! Lesley would be a perfect minister's wife. I thought they might be moving in that direction."

"I don't suppose it would do me any good to say that I like Lesley right where she is, as my executive secretary?"

"Why can't she be both?"

"It seems to me that the Wilsons make a full-time job of this town."

"Have I cheated on my job?" Abbey demanded.

"I was just teasing you."

"Oh."

They faced each other. "I'm a man, Abbey. It has been a long time since I've held a woman. I tease you because I don't want to frighten you with my need. You're not that kind of woman. I have no real desire for that kind of woman, but I am a man.''

Abbey did not reach out and touch him. This was a dangerous moment for them. Her voice was barely above a whisper. ''You go on out. I'll turn the lights off and meet you outside. I know my way by heart.''

His voice drifted back to her as he walked toward the door. ''That could be the story of your life. Someday they'll write on your tombstone, 'She knew her way by heart.' ''

Abbey switched off the lights and stood quietly for a brief moment to get her emotions under control. In her heart she knew Gabe needed more than what he thought he wanted, but he was unaware of that. His denial of his faith had hurt her. She knew that a marriage without shared faith would be a marriage with the heart cut out of it. She sighed. They had a long way to go. They both had wounds to heal before they could come together. She walked through the darkness to the door. The difference between them was that she carried her light within the darkness, while he carried his darkness within.

He was waiting by the door, and she carefully side-stepped his dark form and moved into the cold December night. She didn't see the wry grin on his face, didn't realize that he recognized her precautions. He took the keys from her and locked the door.

''You'll be perfectly safe on your porch,'' he commented. ''I have never tried to kiss a lady who was illuminated by five hundred Christmas lights.''

Abbey laughed in relief. ''It would be like performing in the middle of a neon sign.''

''I don't suppose you might take an orphan in tomorrow?

It's Saturday, and our respective parents will be gone all day. Maybe we could build snow forts. That would be like taking cold showers, wouldn't it? Who could think about romance when they're suffering from frostbite?''

They reached Abbey's front porch. "The people to set up the creche will be here at nine A.M.," she said. "It should only take an hour or so. If it's clear, why don't we go cross-country skiing? You can use Dad's skis. We can make it over to Campbell's Lodge for lunch and be back by late afternoon.''

"Sounds good.'' He kissed her briefly, then sauntered down the steps whistling "Good Night, Ladies.'' He had pressed her keys into her hand during the kiss and she fumbled at the lock, nearly dropping them. Neb made a rush through the door, almost knocking her down. Sheba was close behind. Abbey devoutly hoped that no one was looking out of their windows.

She expected to see Gabe the next morning around ten, but found him waiting at the church door with the Davis family. She was glad she had dressed in her red ski coat with the white fur hood.

Susie Martin had come with Jordan. She and Abbey brought out the sheep while Zeb and Jordan arranged the lights. Gabe ran down to the local store for a replacement floodlight while the other men assembled the stable.

In a short time the Holy Family was established in the stable surrounded by their animal friends. Shepherds and their sheep charged up one side of the small hill in front of the church, while the Magi toiled up the other side.

"I noticed that you put Prodigal out in front.'' Gabe grinned.

"He's special.'' Abbey patted the small black head. "I

always thought of him as the one lost sheep that the shepherd left the other ninety-nine to find.''

They waved the Davis family and friends off and headed toward the porch, where Abbey had placed their skis. Abbey let Neb out for a short run as a precaution and snatched up some dry mittens. Sheba complained vociferously, but Abbey didn't want the gray cat out in the cold all day.

"We have to be back before dark so I can turn on the lights." Abbey let Gabe out into the backyard. "We can walk from here until we get to the corner. Then we have to cross behind the new addition. After that we're in open country."

Gabe adjusted his ski mask, which matched the navyblue trim on his jacket. His eyes had a steely blue sparkle over the mask. Abbey pulled her white mask into place and pushed off.

For two hours they skied across the white fields, following an old creek bed or gliding along a deserted country road. Campbell's Lodge loomed up at the top of a hill on a well-traveled road.

"One good thing," panted Gabe, "it will be downhill when we return."

They leaned their skis and poles against the wall with others and entered the warm lodge. Abbey was delighted to recognize several familiar faces. She ignored the fact that Gabe appeared less than delighted to be included in a crowd scene. He bore his fate with polite civility, especially when several of the men joshed him about his "great battle with Savage Solomon." One man even offered to mate his female with Solomon so that the area could start a new breed of hunting cat. Gabe promised that the man could have his wish, if he could catch Solomon himself. The group roared with glee as the man beat a hasty retreat.

Gabe and Abbey took their places at a table and helped demolish the lunch, which was served family style. The men monopolized Gabe in conversation while the women chatted with Abbey. Abbey thought that Gabe must believe that she had engineered the whole thing. They might as well have had a date in the middle of the town square. Finally, the last of the people drifted away and Gabe escorted Abbey to a couch in front of the big open fire.

"Is there no place in this county where you're not everyone's long-lost cousin?"

"I didn't plan this, honestly."

"I feel like a hound dog trying to cut one little sheep out of the herd. Every time I think I have you corralled, the herd moves in. Is your whole life always this full of people?"

Abbey admired the fit of his blue ski sweater over the broad shoulders. He had joked about the uphill climb to the lodge, but he was obviously physically fit. She regretted that they would have to leave soon in order to reach home before dark. It had been disappointing to be constantly surrounded by people at the lodge. It could have been a very romantic place for a couple alone.

"Not always. You should know better than most." Abbey sipped her cider demurely, fearing that her blush would match her scarlet sweater.

"Are there any more things at home to paint?" he inquired hopefully.

"Nope." Abbey didn't look at him.

"We could make up something new to paint."

"We can talk here."

He slid down on the couch so that his long legs reached the hearth. "Yes, ma'am. I guess I should be grateful that there are no mountains in Iowa, or we'd be climbing them. What do you do with dates in the summer? No, don't tell me. You go scuba-diving and water-skiing. I assume all of your boyfriends are Olympic-class athletes."

"I don't have that many boyfriends."

"Why not? Are they lying beside the road in exhaustion, waiting for a good Samaritan to come along and rescue them from your rather grueling courtship?"

"If you're that tired, maybe we can get a ride home."

"Perish the thought! They may find my bones in one of those fields come next spring. Just remember that I tried to keep up."

"Seriously, Gabe. We have to leave soon to get home before dark. If you think it's too much in one day . . ."

He rose and looked down at her sardonically. "Let's put it this way, Abbey. It's more entertaining than cold showers. Your blush does look charming with the red sweater. Come on. Once more unto the breach, dear Abbey."

Gabe was not exhausted by the trip home, but Abbey was. He had been joking about his stamina, because she was hard put to keep up with him. By the time they made it to her backyard, her legs were jelly and her breath was coming in ragged gasps. She rested on the back steps and watched him prop their skis against the house.

He looked at her pointedly. "Can I help you in?"

"First take the keys and go turn on the manger lights. I want Dad to see it when he comes home."

He strode off through the snow while Abbey struggled to her feet and opened the back door. Neb rushed out in his usual frenzy while Sheba complained loudly about being locked inside all day. Abbey staggered into the living room and turned on the porch lights. She reversed her path and put on some coffee. She had just fallen into a kitchen chair when Gabe entered with Neb.

Neb careened around them, doing a clog dance on their feet until Gabe found some dog food and fed him. Sheba yowled to be let in, and Gabe performed the same service for her. Abbey sat with her head resting on her arms on the table. A coffee cup appeared before her and the rich aroma revived her flagging spirits.

"Revenge is sweet," murmured Gabe, sitting down at the table. "Think of all the would-be suitors you left in the dust. A little of your own medicine won't hurt you."

Abbey glared at him over her coffee cup. "It wasn't supposed to be an endurance trial, Mr. Kendall. It was just a little old cross-country hike."

He leaned toward her so that they were almost nose to nose across the table. "I love the way your eyes go black when you feel strongly about something."

"Glory. First you tease me about suitors I don't have, then you nearly kill me off in revenge for those imaginary suitors. On top of all that, you tell me how black my eyes are, when they're brown. It's been quite a day."

He put one hand behind her neck and kissed her. The kiss was almost frightening in its intensity, considering there was a table between them. Only one of his hands touched her, while both of hers were on the table. The kiss had a kind of hunger in it that was frightening. She tried to draw back, but his hand held her like iron. She felt as though she would lose consciousness if he didn't let her go. Abruptly he released her, and she knew a sense of loss. That had not been the kiss of the gentle man she had known until now, but something else entirely. It had held the threat of something unleashed.

His eyes drilled into hers. A darkness grew in them and Abbey knew she was seeing Gabe without his usual mask.

Gabe despised himself for kissing her. For one moment the fury and terrible need in him had overcome his control. He looked at Abbey's stricken face. Her lips were swollen from the kiss. How desperately he wanted to lose himself in her loving, to forget his past. A suffocating guilt descended on him. The smallest chance at happiness always brought the furies of remembrance down upon his shoulders. He didn't fully realize how much of his pain he had shared with Abbey in that kiss, but he knew he had frightened her. He hated himself for causing her pain. He hated himself for so much, it was a cruelty for him even to be around the goodness that was Abbey. He was like a man who had been led from the desert to a cool, fresh spring but was not able to drink from it.

With horror, Abbey watched the emotions flicker across Gabe's face like lightning flashes. Self-hatred, defeat and despair were mirrored in the blue-black of his eyes. She was being pulled into the vortex of a whirlpool of black, oily water. Abbey knew with a deadly certainty that she was witnessing the struggle of Gabe's spirit. She knew that this was the battle he had been fighting for over two years. Her hands reached out to him to help alleviate that dreadful loneliness, but he pushed himself back and away from her.

"Don't, Abbey!" Anguish gave a bite to his voice. "Don't let me contaminate you. I have no right to touch you. Don't let me inflict myself on you."

Abbey rose to go around the table and take him in her arms to soothe him. He pulled away from her and headed toward the door.

''No, Abbey!'' The edge of his voice was even sharper than before. He slammed out of the house.

Abbey stood with an aching heart until the receding sound of his car's engine told her he was gone. Silent tears ran down her face. Neb thrust his muzzle into her hand, whining in sympathy. Her tears dropped onto his brown fur, but she was helpless to stop them.

Absently she stroked his damp head to stop his whimpering. The day had gone so well. It had woven itself into companionship and laughter like a shimmering cloth, only to be ripped apart in shreds at the end. She breathed slowly, letting the tortured muscles that had contracted in the last few minutes relax to a dull ache. She felt a satisfaction in the pain, as though she had eased some of his. She knew that if she was to help this man, there would be more pain ahead.

Chapter Eight

Having had little sleep the night before, Abbey spent Sunday morning in a kind of weary haze. Amy and Emil dropped over for lunch after church, which kept her too busy to think much about Gabe. She had talked to Ralph at church, but Gabe hadn't attended services.

"Are you catching a cold?" Amy washed the last pan and handed it to Abbey to dry. "You look awfully tired, not to mention a little ragged around the edges."

Abbey changed the subject easily. "I thought Ross was coming with you."

"He had to go to the Kendalls' for dinner. You know they hired Ginny Scarpino, Mama's oldest, as their cook, so they're eating well. Ginny said the only one she really cooks for is Ralph. Gabe doesn't eat much of anything on the rare occasions when he's actually home." Amy shot Abbey a sharp look. "Ginny reported that he spent the weekend working at the church. I understand that he worked all day Saturday.''

"We set up the manger scene in the morning and then went cross-country skiing to Campbell's.'' Abbey answered the unspoken question.

"Have a good time?'' Amy was elaborately casual.

"The skiing was fun.'' Abbey evaded, putting away the pans.

Much to Abbey's relief, a knock on the door interrupted Amy's cross-examination. They opened the door to find Ross standing in a soft flurry of snowflakes. "Can you girls come out and play?''

They pulled him into the kitchen to shake off the snow like a friendly puppy. "The girl scouts are having a bazaar in the town hall. I thought you two might want to hunt up some Christmas presents. I'm here to act as your honorable escort.'' He assayed a low bow.

"You two go scout the territory and report back,'' Abbey punned badly. "I have work to do at home.''

After she'd convinced Ross and Amy to go without her, Abbey waved them off into the gently falling snow, trying not to envy their obvious happiness. She rejoiced for Amy and Ross and the changes that love had brought them. Amy seemed so much softer, and Ross was taking a real interest in the town since Amy had introduced him to people and helped him share their activities. They were good for each other. Amy had revealed over lunch that Ross would escort her to church next Sunday. In Counsel that amounted to a preannouncement of an engagement. She smiled as the two figures swept down the street, smiling into each other's eyes, oblivious of the outside world.

Emil and Ira had both dozed off over the Sunday paper

while digesting their large meal. Abbey attempted to work on some of her ever present Christmas lists, but her mind kept straying. Finally she tiptoed past the sleeping men and threw on her red ski jacket. Neb was delighted at the prospect of a walk. Pulling on warm red mittens and boots, she let the animals out into the snow.

She thought she might join Amy and Ross at the bazaar, but realized that she really wanted to be alone with her thoughts in the soft peace of this white world. Neb frolicked about her feet, rushing away to investigate a squirrel or a human acquaintance and then reporting back to Abbey. Without being aware of it, Abbey had walked to the edge of town where the old cemetery was located. Here lay three generations of Wilsons, from her mother to her great-grandfather. She brushed off a marble bench near the family plot and sat facing the graves of her ancestors. There were the graves of Josiah and Naomi, with their marble angel watching over them. There was their oldest son, who had died of typhoid fever at the age of fifteen. There were their four other children, who had died with their mother in the influenza epidemic. There were the tiny graves of the babies who had never known life at all. Of the eight children borne by Naomi, only one had lived to adulthood. Had Abbey's grandfather, Samuel, wanted to stay in Counsel all of his life? Abbey wondered if he had remained to please his father, who had lost his wife and other children. What if Samuel had wanted to be a riverboat pilot like Mark Twain, or a pioneer in the old West? Had a sense of duty kept Samuel here?

She didn't see the figure in the dark coat until Neb whisked away from her side to welcome him. Gabe sat down beside her. "Am I intruding?"

She couldn't keep the happiness from flooding her heart, but she tried to discipline her voice. "Not at all. I was just thinking of the past." She shared some of her thoughts about her grandfather.

"History repeating itself?"

"I don't know," Abbey said pensively. "I know that I wouldn't demand that my children follow in my footsteps. Of course, if I'd been a man, I might have ended up in the seminary out of the same sense of duty. My father loves being a pastor. It isn't duty with him, he really has a vocation. I can hardly remember my grandfather, though. Mostly I was thinking about the women. How terrible to lose so many children. It must have been difficult for Samuel and Josiah to have been the only survivors. Even so, they never lost their faith. Their belief was never shaken."

"How do you know what went on in the secret part of their hearts?"

"I don't, of course, but I just feel that their faith saw them through."

"Or their sense of duty."

"Or both."

He tucked a stray lock of hair back into her hood. "Or both. I left my father at your house. He, Emil, and Ira were settling down to a game of Monopoly. It will probably last at least until evening. I feel sorry for Ira, caught between those two."

"Don't worry. Dad always wins at Monopoly. You don't live on a shoestring budget without being shrewd about how to spend money to the best advantage. Wait and see."

He touched one of the red mittens. "I'm glad to see you

wearing the right kind of gloves for a change. I wanted to see you alone for a moment to apologize for yesterday. I didn't mean to alarm you. You looked like Jane Eyre facing Mr. Rochester. I didn't want you to be afraid to come to work tomorrow.''

Abbey steeled herself and faced him. "I wasn't frightened, Gabe, not for myself. I was terrified for what I saw happening to you. Your pain hurt me because I hate to see you suffer. I'm not a little girl to be shielded from a man's need and loneliness. You once compared me to a rose, but you don't seem to realize how strong a rose is here. It survives bitter cold and ice. It finds a niche on old fences, barns or walls, and blooms. A rose is tenacious, sturdy and tough. You seem to want women to be frail flowers that have to be nurtured in the shade or in hothouses. You keep forcing that image on me and I can't, and won't, try to fit it.''

Gabe looked so surprised that Abbey nearly lost her courage. "I don't mean to shock you, Gabe, but I do think you need to bring your outlook up to date. You've heard us tease Ross about how little he knows about small-town living. He didn't learn anything because he limited himself to the factory or his motel room. Amy has introduced him to different facets of the town, and he's enjoying the people and the experience. You knew one woman, you admitted that yourself. I understand that your Ann was a lovely, fragile person, but all of us are not violets in the shade of our manly oaks. Some of us work for a living. Many of us are more open and outspoken than Ann was. That doesn't make either of us wrong, it just makes us different. I am no less womanly because I'm not afraid to speak up for myself.

I'm not ashamed of what I am, although I know I have many faults. I see you as you are, without comparing you to anyone else. Why can't you see me as I really am?''

''I seem to have offended you,'' Gabe said stiffly.

''That's a cop-out, Gabriel Kendall. You do that whenever someone shows you that she honestly cares, particularly if she cares enough to tell you the truth.''

Abbey saw his eyes darken as they had the day before, and her heart quailed within her. She didn't know if she could face that again. Her love and faith gave her the courage to go on.

''Look at those graves. Don't you think loving was painful for those people? Naomi bore eight children. Two died at birth. Her eldest died of typhoid. Four were lost in the same flu epidemic that took her. Only one son and his father survived. They could have given up. They could have cursed God, and died, as Job's wife told him to do, but they didn't. This town is a monument to their love and faith. You loved Ann and your children, so you must believe that love exists. Death doesn't separate us from loving. Don't you see? It's because my father loved my mother so much that their marriage was good. That's why my father will have the faith to love again. Life isn't a children's game. You don't just get mad at God for giving you a bad turn, and quit living.''

''Why can't I?'' snarled Gabe, glaring into her eyes. ''You're right about Ann. She was a lady, a vulnerable and loving woman. She was perfect. She was everything to me. What do you know about loving? You're so busy doing good deeds that you've never stopped to settle down and love one man. What can you possibly understand about the agony of having your heart torn out of you while you're still alive! Have you ever had to pack away the belongings of your loved ones? Every room has memories. You think you see them laughing on the stairs and hear small feet running behind you. You turn to pick them up and no one is there. My father was in the hospital because of me. I was alone—alone because of a vicious gust of wind from a storm that shouldn't have happened. The weather reports said it would be clear. Ann didn't want to go without me, but I told her to go ahead and not be silly. Those were my last words to her, 'Don't be silly'! One day I have a wife, two beautiful children, a mother and brother. The next day I have only my father, whom I have crippled with my own words.''

He turned away from her and stared over the graveyard. ''I loved them more than my life. He took their lives instead of mine. I will never forgive Him for that. Never!''

A dead silence punctuated Gabe's statement. Abbey struggled up through layers of empathetic anguish for him. Let me reach him, she prayed. She took off her mittens so that she could take one of his hands in hers. He neither pulled it away nor responded. She knew he was a great distance from her.

''You were right about me.'' Abbey stumbled a little over the words. ''I have never known what it is to lose a partner. I have lost a mother, so I can understand that loss. I had no brothers or sisters to lose. I can't imagine the agony of giving up a child to death. You are far more fortunate than I have been.''

She felt a shudder go through him at her use of the word ''fortunate.''

''Because you did know that loving. You did hold your children in your arms. You found a mate to fulfill that longing in yourself. Even though it was all taken from you, Gabe, you've had what I have never had, and may never be given. My arms are empty.

"Perhaps you're right. I'm too quick to speak out on what is none of my business. That is a terrible failing in me. Please don't judge the Master by this poor servant. My father would be able to help far more than I, but it seems as though I'm always the only one around when you open a door, so I put my big foot in it and make matters worse. Please forgive me."

His hand closed around hers. She brought it up to her cheek. "We aren't perfect. We bumble about doing all sorts of harm to each other. Please believe that I was only trying to help. I won't ask you to forget the past. You could not, and should not, forget. I'm asking you to go on. Pick up your life. Look around and start again. It will never be the same, but there are many kinds of loving possible in a life."

"Where does all this wisdom come from?" Gabe's voice was hoarse with emotion.

Abbey took his other hand until he faced her. "From my heart."

His hands closed on hers and he looked down at them, avoiding her eyes. "I would like to promise you that I will try, or make some kind of noble declaration to you, Abbey. But I cannot believe that this cripple will walk again. I must warn you to put that caring heart of yours in someone else's keeping. I come back to you over and over again to warm my cold soul with your generosity. By now it must be obvious to you that I have no warmth to give you. You can give me a semblance of living. With you I can laugh and almost enjoy life. You build me up each day, but what you accomplish is torn down each night. Yesterday I forced you to share some of that. I don't want to subject you to that again. I won't chain you to the nightmare that is my life. I haven't fallen that low."

Abbey brushed her cheek against his dark hair. "There's no time limit, is there? Let it happen in your own time, in your own season."

She didn't point out to him that he had refused to forgive the Lord for taking his family. She had laid to rest one of her worst fears about him. You can't be angry with someone you do not believe in; therefore, Gabe must believe. Her eyes blurred in gratitude.

He stood, pulling her up with him. "It's time to go home. Your hands are like ice." He retrieved her mittens and whistled for Neb. The door was closed once more, but today it had opened wider than ever before.

The next week was trying. Even Lesley commented that Gabe was being "more Kendall than usual." She shook her head at the closed door of his office.

"Maybe it's because it's only two weeks until Christmas. I know that's the worst time for me to be alone. You remember so many painful things at Christmastime."

"Not this Christmas." Abbey hugged the smaller woman. "You'll be too busy helping us out at the church. Don't forget you promised to make your special glazed ham for dinner."

Lesley hugged her back. "Wait until you taste my apple cobbler."

Abbey had expected Gabe to pull back into himself after their Sunday discussion, and she wasn't disappointed. She threw herself into her work and the pre-Christmas activities at the church, relieved that the cannery employees had voted for a bonus rather than a party. She didn't think she could face another party just now.

She missed Amy's companionship. Ross took up all of Amy's free time, which was as it should be. It was the lack of cheerful patter in her life that reminded her of Amy's absence.

Wednesday night found Lesley and Abbey finishing up the angel gowns for the Sunday school choir; tomorrow was dress rehearsal. They'd been hard at work since leaving the cannery. Ira was attending choir rehearsal, so the ladies were free to spread out their material, machines and tinsel from the kitchen to the living room. By nine the mothers had left to pick up their children from rehearsal and go home. Lesley and Abbey were just putting the last hem in a tiny robe when a knock at the back door interrupted them.

Abbey got up from the floor and shook tinsel from her jeans and one of Ira's old shirts. She pushed her hair back up into a topknot held precariously by a red ribbon and threw open the door.

Gabe stood there extending a pair of red mittens. "You do have a problem with gloves, don't you?"

A moment later, Ira arrived home, hungry but delighted to see both Lesley and Gabe. The ladies picked up their mess while Ira and Gabe rummaged in the kitchen, coming up with thick sandwiches and slightly burned cocoa. The food revived Ira, who suggested that they decorate the bare tree that had been residing in their living room since the week before.

"Tomorrow is a workday," Abbey reminded Ira.

"It won't take very long," he cajoled.

Lesley and Abbey looked at each other in commiseration. "Men!"

It was midnight before the tree was completed. Ira and Gabe had to string the lights perfectly. Each strand was checked for burned-out bulbs and put on the tree as though it were a permanent addition to the house. After the lights were up, the two men fell exhaustedly onto the sofa. They let the women finish the tree, giving suggestions and comments through mouthfuls of gingerbread that Abbey had stirred up for the evening's snack.

Abbey had been somewhat dubious about having Gabe help with the tree, fearing it would resurrect unhappy memories. As always, he surprised her. No shadows crossed his eyes; no misunderstandings or hauntings seemed to influence him. It was an extremely pleasant evening. Abbey put it down to Ira's presence. Gabe had said that he would keep coming even though he had nothing to give her. Was that what he was doing tonight? He was carefully correct. It was as though he were playing the part of a considerate friend of the family come for a visit. There was no hint of personal feelings between himself and Abbey. He treated her exactly as a brother would treat a younger sister. It was only when he accidentally touched her fingers when handing her a cup that a hint of his true feelings warmed her. It was a slight pressure, but heat crossed her palm and spread up her arm like electricity. He was letting her know that he could play this part, but nothing had changed. How many masks did Gabe have? How many had she not yet seen?

Later that night she had trouble falling asleep. In the few hours before dawn she found that Gabe had even invaded her dreams. In her dream she was searching for him in a woods. It was an old, dark forest, full of fearsome shapes. Abbey had a lantern in her hand. She knew she couldn't lose it or the darkness would overwhelm her. She held the light before her and called his name over and over. At last she saw him in a clearing, but he was surrounded by dark forms that seemed to be pulling at him and tormenting him. Abbey ran to help him. Swinging her lantern at the figures that swirled around him, she forced them to retreat back into the shadows. Abbey tried to take him in her arms as he fell to his knees, but she saw that he was not looking at her but behind her. She turned in the slow-motion way that people do in dreams and saw three figures—a young woman and two tiny children. She knew immediately who they were.

Lesley's voice in the dream came to her from a distance. "He never cried for them. That's why they are here. He won't let them go because he never grieved for them. Please help him, Abbey."

Abbey awoke to the sound of her own sobbing. "I'm trying! I'm trying!"

Her bedside light switched on. Ira stood beside her bed in his old flannel robe. "You haven't had nightmares since you were little and you saw that old Disney film about Ichabod Crane."

Abbey sat up and brushed away the tears with the back of her hands. "This was a little different, Dad."

Ira sat on the edge of the bed. "Abbey, I'm not blind. You look peaked. Would you like to share the dream?"

Abbey looked into his dear eyes and explained her nightmare. When she was finished, he shook his head.

"It's logical. You do not handle grief by ignoring it. Lesley's mentioned this to me, of course. She's a wise woman. Grief isn't something that goes away just because you pretend it isn't there. Gabe has to come to terms with his grief and his guilt.''

"What could he possibly be guilty about?"

"All survivors feel guilty, Abbey. There are several stages in grief, you know. Gabe's refusal to face his grief will not let him go on to live with it. Actually, his situation is more complicated than that. His father's illness has added more guilt. By the way, Ralph doesn't blame Gabe, and he's tried to talk to his son, but Gabe avoids the subject.''

"You seem to know all about it." Abbey hadn't realized the extent of Ira's knowledge.

"Ralph is worried. Gabe is the last of his family. Ralph was very lonely until he came here. It's as though Gabe, by ignoring his own pain, refuses to recognize his father's right to grieve also.''

"I hadn't thought of that."

"No, because you think only of Gabe. You've done that from the first day you met him.''

"Dad!"

"I didn't plan on talking with you at four in the morning, but it's as good a time as any. I don't think you'll be getting much more sleep tonight. Please understand, my dear. If you had met and fallen in love with Gabe Kendall three or four years ago, I would have been delighted. The Kendalls were a strong, loving family. It would have been ideal for you, in my eyes. But now . . .''

"Dad, you said to let the Lord work it out."

"I know I did. Are you sure that's what you're doing? It seems to me that you're giving Him an awful lot of help.''

"No more than I would give to anyone in need. My loving Gabe or not wouldn't change my duty to help him, would it?''

"Abbey, please don't bandy words with me."

"I love him, Dad. I didn't mean to. I only meant to help, but I fell in love with him."

Ira looked sad. "I had hoped you would have a joyous courtship. I wanted you to be cherished and cared for. This is one of the times when your mother's loss is keenly felt; she would have known what to say to you. I don't want to put Gabe down. It isn't that I don't care for him—I love him as I loved his parents, but I love you more. I would be failing in my duty to you as a parent if I didn't point out the problems of loving a man who may never allow himself to return your love. Even if he married you, Abbey, I'm afraid you would always feel somewhat cheated."

"I wouldn't marry him unless he was free to love me and had been reconciled once more with the family of God. I promise you that, Dad. There could be no marriage without those two things."

"I'm relieved to hear that, but I can't help but foresee a rocky road ahead. I know you found Jordan less than exciting, but he would have cared for you."

"I'd have failed Jordan in the same way you're talking about Gabe failing me. You wouldn't have wanted that, Dad."

"How will you feel if it doesn't work out, Abbey?"

Abbey tried to face his question honestly. She had deliberately avoided thinking about a future without Gabe. It was too dreadful to contemplate, but she didn't want to worry her father any further. She answered him with the only truth she knew.

"I will face that when it happens, if it happens. Have faith in all that you and Mom have taught me, Dad. How would you have felt if you had lost Mother at my age?"

"It would have sorely tried my faith, but I would have gone on, grateful that someone like her had lived at all. Her existence and goodness in this world would have been sufficient for me. I would have missed the joy of having her as my partner. I would never have known the sharing of our love with our child. However, for me, it would be hard to think of having missed knowing Elizabeth, even to save myself pain. You knew what my answer to that would be, daughter."

"Do you want me to give you an answer that is any less honest? I love him, Dad. The world for me is better because he is here."

"Even if he can never be whole again?"

"Even then."

Quietly Ira kissed her forehead and left the room. There was no more for him to say. He could not deny her love, because he would never have denied his own. He could only pray for her as he had every day of her life.

As Abbey watched the dawn filter through her window she ached in body and spirit. This wasn't a good beginning for the day. Yesterday had never ended. She crawled out of bed. Sheba yowled at being disturbed in her sleep.

"Me too," sighed Abbey as Sheba meowed at her. "Me too!"

Chapter Nine

Ross, you didn't!" Amy exclaimed in horror.

"It kept them quiet, didn't it?" Ross looked innocent.

Amy turned to Abbey in disgust. "He gave all twenty of the sheep chewing gum!"

"Sheep chew cud like cows, don't they? What's the harm?" asked Ross.

Abbey handed Ross a paper cup. "They have to sing about being little lost sheep. Can't you hear the chorus now? Baaa. Chomp. Baaa. Chomp. Baaa."

Grinning, Ross took the cup and went off to collect the gum from the sheep.

"It is funny." Abbey smiled. "I don't think the chorus leader would find it amusing, but the parents would love it."

"I should have put him in charge of the shepherds."

Amy shook her head. "I thought those sheep were too quiet."

Abbey's own group of angels was called and she left to herd them upstairs. All of the helpers slipped into the back pews to catch the end of the program, which included the entire Sunday school.

Abbey sat in the back of the old church and thought about how new the program was every year. The beautiful voices of the adult choir filled the church with glorious sound on Sundays, but the children brought a freshness to everything they did. From the tiny trebles of the babies in the group to the uncertain basses of the teenage boys, she was enchanted. What was it about the young that appealed to her? Abbey caught the glances of several proud parental eyes with tears in them. They all gazed sentimentally at each other. Ross and Amy were sitting beside her, holding hands. Their faces had the same doting expression as the parents.

Everyone stood to sing the last hymn with the children. "O Come, All Ye Faithful" thundered through the church and filtered out onto the main street of Counsel. Gabe Kendall sat in his car and listened to the old strains of his childhood. He knew Abbey was inside, but he couldn't bring himself to join her. He resisted the welcome of the church lights to sit in his lonely car and wait.

His mouth was a grim line as he ignored the happy crowd pouring out of the church after the program. Children's voices floated above the adults'. His hands tightened on the steering wheel. This was precisely the kind of situation he avoided at all costs, but his need to see Abbey outweighed his strong aversion.

It had been a rough week. His conversation with Abbey

in the cemetery had been more disturbing than he would admit. He was functioning as efficiently as always at the factory, but his private life was falling apart. His visit to the Wilsons' on Wednesday had eased the pain for an evening. He was afraid that Abbey was fast becoming an addiction. He wanted to be in her comforting presence. He didn't even pretend to have an excuse anymore. Like a lost puppy, he showed up on Abbey's doorstep, and she took him in. He frowned at the sad image, but knew it was close to the truth.

In half an hour the crowd had dwindled to a trickle of people who were fading into the night. Gabe decided to meet Abbey at the church door. Maybe he could talk her into going out for coffee. Getting out of the car, he headed toward the church basement door.

Abbey was chatting with Jenny Payne, who was wrestling with her toddler while waiting for her five-year-old "angel." She groaned as one sturdy two-year-old foot inadvertently kicked her in the stomach.

"Give him to me, Jenny," Abbey offered. "He's too hot in that snowsuit. I'll take him outside while you find Jamie."

Jenny handed the baby over with undisguised relief. "Knowing Jamie, she's taken off with that little Scarpino kid. Those two are a public nuisance when they get together."

Abbey laughed, thinking of how people used to say the same thing about her and Amy when they were little. She lifted the baby and smiled into his big blue eyes as she pulled up the hood of his snowsuit.

"Mama," he pronounced. All women were "Mama" to him.

"Oh, don't I wish!" Abbey kissed him and led him out

the door. They stepped into the brightness of the outdoor Christmas lights.

The baby staggered over to the snowdrift by the walk. "No! No!" He patted the snow and looked inquiringly at Abbey. "No?"

"Oh, snow! Right. That's snow."

"No," agreed the baby wisely, then wheeled around and tottered down the sidewalk away from the church. Abbey was in close pursuit. She saw the figure of a man coming toward her, but because of the glare of the lights, she was unable to make out his features.

"Catch him, please!" she called.

To Abbey's relief the dark form swept the baby up in his arms. She ran up to him. "Thanks. He just tore off and . . ."

"Dada," chirped the baby.

Gabe Kendall stepped into the pool of light and thrust the baby at Abbey. She cuddled him to her, but the child preferred the higher vantage point of the man's arms and leaned away from her. He put his arms out to Gabe and cried, "Dada!" His small hands in their fuzzy mittens reached for the man.

Gabe's eyes seemed to break into fragments of blue glass. The pupils expanded, almost covering the shattered blue. He stepped back with the slow, jerky motions of a sleepwalker. His hands fell to his sides.

Abbey tried to handle the child, who kept throwing himself toward Gabe. "Dada! Dada! Dada!"

Gabe shuddered as though the baby's voice were a sword going through his body.

"Gabe! Wait!" Abbey couldn't let go of the baby, but she knew the child's voice was torturing him. "Wait. I'll be back in a minute.'' She ran back into the church. Luckily, the baby's mother was coming with Jamie in tow. She handed Jenny her child, excused herself hastily and dashed back to where she had left Gabe. He was gone. Not surprised, she hesitated, wondering where he would head for. She hurried to the rectory, praying that he might have gone there to wait for her. Only Neb was in residence.

She searched the street with frantic eyes. His car was nowwhere to be seen. Abbey slid into Ira's car and pulled out of the drive. Would he go to the factory to bury himself in work, as he had done so often in the past? No car in the lot. No lights in his window. Abbey drove toward the edge of town, past the old cemetery where they had talked last Sunday. She continued down the old road to the Johnson place. Thankfully she pulled up beside his car. He had gone home! She ran up the steps and knocked on the door. It was answered by a worried Ralph.

''Mr. Kendall.'' Abbey tried not to sound too anxious, not wanting to upset the older man. He was looking haggard as it was.

Without preamble he pointed up the stairs. ''The attic, I think.''

Abbey was grateful to him for not asking questions. She sprinted up the steps to the second floor and on up to the attic door. She turned the knob and found it locked. She almost pounded on the door in frustration, but instead, drew a calming breath and called his name. No answer. She knocked, but still received no response. Then she remembered playing with the Johnson girls. One day the youngest had locked herself in the attic. The others had simply used a key from one of the bedroom doors. The keys were interchangeable.

She rushed down the stairs to search the locks of the doors on the second floor. A small room that was once the Johnson sewing room yielded a key. Once more she was at the door. The lock turned and she stepped into the attic. She was temporarily blinded until her eyes became accustomed to the dim light coming in the eyebrow windows from the outside security lamps. She could just make out his profile against the window. She stumbled into an old trunk and sat down before her knees gave way completely. He was here. She was here. Now the time element didn't seem so crucial. Somehow she knew that it was terribly important that she be there for him.

His face was ashen in the dim light, his eyes deeply shadowed. Abbey could see that he was kneeling in front of a trunk with his hands grasping its sides. His voice was dull.

"Ann began filling this trunk when we were first married. She said it would hold the memories of all the years for us to enjoy when we grew old. See, our picture album is on top." Gabe's voice droned on, listing the treasured memorabilia packed by a loving young wife and mother. A change was creeping into the dark voice. He slammed the lid of the trunk closed.

"You want me to forget them! How can I? Take up my life, you said. What life do I have to take up? They were my life! How can I forget when every child I see reminds me? You were so quick to tell me how others had suffered and went on. What did they go on to?"

Abbey accepted his anger, knowing that it was not she at whom the rage was directed.

"I can't accept it. I don't want to accept it. What do I have left if they're gone?" His voice caught, and Abbey's heart wrenched. "I believed in God. Ann believed in Him utterly. My two innocent children. Where was He? Where was He when they died? Why didn't God at least have the compassion to take me with them? Why did I have to be left behind? You ask Him, since you know Him so well! He's a stranger to me."

Abbey's heart filled and overflowed with love for him. She thought of how hard it had been for Ira and herself to recover from the death of her mother even with the sure knowledge of God's love. How had this man survived at all? How had he managed to hold on to his sanity, let alone care for his father and run a business? It was a measure of his character that he had wandered in this desert alone and not given up.

The deep voice was heavy with implacable intensity, demanding an answer from her that she prayed would be what he needed to hear. "Where was He?"

Abbey heard her own voice as if it belonged to someone else. Somewhere from the well that was herself and her faith came a slow, sweet voice full of compassion. "Where were we when His son died on Calvary to save us? What promises did you accept as a Christian, Gabe? You said you believed, but you refuse to believe that eternity is more important than death. Your family had the faith you lack. They are forever safe, much safer than we are now. We have to go on and earn our way back home. Dearest Gabe, they are already there. You and I grieve because we are left behind. It's selfish. We want them back for our own sakes, even though we know in our hearts that what they have is better. They're free. They'll never suffer again. You're still here because your work is not finished. Life is a journey. Deny your faith, and you condemn yourself to struggle through the world without light. You know the truth, but you want to run away from it. Do you really believe He loves you less because He made it harder for you? Doesn't it occur to you that the Lord may love you more to give you a heavier burden to bear?''

''What am I?'' Gabe's voice was barely above a whisper. ''I am nothing.''

Abbey gently put her arms around him. ''I used to wear a button when I was a kid in Sunday school. It said, 'God doesn't make junk!' ''

Gabe started to laugh, and choked, and suddenly the laughter turned to sobs. Deep, wrenching sobs shook his body as the tears that had been suppressed for over two years spilled over from his soul. Abbey held him and rocked him in the age-old position of solace.

''I loved them so much,'' he wept. ''I loved them so much.'' She held him, sharing his grief until he became exhausted and they sat in silence. He raised his head from her shoulder and sighed. ''My father. He can't go to bed without my help.''

She knew he didn't want to come out into the brightly lit hallway with her. He wished to be alone for a few moments to compose himself before he went to his father.

''I have to go.'' She stood and picked up her coat, which had fallen behind the trunk. ''I'll tell him that you'll be down in a few minutes.''

''Thank you.''

Abbey slipped out of the attic and went down the stairs to reassure a worried Ralph. ''He's fine,'' she said. ''He had to grieve, you see. He thought he could go on forever without acknowledging his pain. Now he understands that he needs to mourn.''

Ralph held her hand. "I know. I've always known. Now he will heal."

"He wanted me to tell you that he would be down soon." Abbey squeezed Ralph's hand comfortingly, then started for the door.

"Abbey."

"Mr. Kendall?"

"You love my son?"

"Yes."

"You know he may never forgive you for having seen him give in to his emotions."

"I know."

"We Kendalls are a stiff-necked clan. Our pride is our worst enemy."

"My father says that is true of all humankind."

"We have a larger dose of it than most. I just wanted to warn you that you may have saved him, only to lose him."

"I realize that."

"I'm sorry, Abbey."

"It's all right. It was my choice. I accept the consequences. The problem with loving is that you have to do what is right for the one you love. It goes with the territory, I guess."

"Thank you, Abbey."

Abbey made it out the door before she burst into tears. She fell into the car and automatically started it, refusing to let herself think until she reached the sanctuary of her home. Tears rained down her face continually, but she deliberately blanked out her mind and doggedly headed the car down the highway into Counsel. At the town limits she slowed down and finally pulled into her own driveway. Wearily she crawled from behind the wheel of the car and dragged herself into the house. Ira was waiting for her. He divested her of her coat and purse and gently pushed her toward the stairs.

"Ralph called me. Go to bed. Sleep. There is nothing more you can do tonight."

Without a word, she obeyed her father. The tears of fatigue and anxiety still stained her face when the bed rose up to meet her.

Abbey did not waken until after noon. She bathed and dressed in her old jeans and a warm flannel shirt. There was a note from Ira on the kitchen table. "Going to Millicent's for lunch with Lesley. Join us, if you wake up in time." Abbey shook her head with a tremulous smile. She wouldn't be the best company today. She was glad it was too late to join them. Those three people knew her far too well. She poured herself a cup of coffee and curled up in the old arm chair facing the Christmas tree. She felt the lethargy that comes after serious trauma. Her mind was disoriented, filled with thoughts and events that chased themselves around helter-skelter. She felt a kind of separation from them, as though she had been only an onlooker at last night's happenings. She leaned back in the old chair and tried to organize her thoughts, but they eluded her attempts at discipline. Her eyes felt scratchy, and she closed them to ease the dryness. Sleep overcame her once more. The cup fell unnoticed to the carpet.

That was how Amy found her. When she had called earlier, Ira had warned her that Abbey was under the weather and might be in bed. Amy had tiptoed into the house through the back door because she didn't want to disturb her friend if she was asleep. She didn't knock because she knew Abbey would get up and answer the door. She was shocked by Abbey's appearance.

Deep circles traced shadows under her eyes. Abbey's ivory skin now had a translucent quality that distressed Amy. The cheekbones were more prominent than ever before. Concerned about how tired Abbey looked, Amy picked up the fallen cup, determined to leave without waking her. But the brown eyes opened immediately, and the familiar gleam of welcome held Amy there.

"Why didn't you wake me up?"

"You looked like you needed the sleep."

"There's coffee on the stove," Abbey invited. "I guess I'm just feeling a little forlorn. You look gorgeous in that red coat."

Amy tossed the coat over the sofa and went to get the coffee. When she came back, she was pleased to see that some color had returned to Abbey's pale face, but she still looked extremely tired.

"Why don't you go back to bed and let me bring you some hot soup? I warned you last Sunday that you were looking ragged. You must be coming down with something nasty." Amy frowned at.

"Don't worry. You know I'm rarely sick. It's just been a busy week."

Amy sat down, pinning Abbey with her silver eyes. "You work too hard, too long and too much, Abbey Wilson. You can't work at the cannery and take Elizabeth's place, too. Remember, your mother made the church a full-time job. No one can work two full-time jobs and be good at both unless she wants to wind up in bed."

"It's not the work, Amy. Believe me, I am not over-worked."

"You could fool me. I know you're seeing Gabe Kendall, but if you ask me, he's not much fun. It must be like trying to relax with the statue of *The Thinker*. I'm sure he's an admirable man, but he's very trying."

"Amy!" Abbey remonstrated.

"Abbey. Does it occur to you that his high standards are just plain male egotism? He is so impossibly perfect." She held up her hand to stop Abbey's protest. "I know. I know. You're going to tell me how tragic his life has been. Agreed. But your life hasn't exactly been a picnic. Honey, why can't you have some of the good things in life? Why fall for a glacier like Gabe Kendall? He's an iceberg that may never thaw. You could die of frostbite around him. I don't want to be cruel, but I don't want to see you hurt, either. What's wrong with falling in love with someone who loves you back? Find someone without ghosts in his life. Let Gabe live in his past. Don't muck up your future with him!"

Amy paused for breath, a little ashamed of her outburst. "Hey, I didn't come here to lecture you. It's just that I'm so happy that I want you to be happy, too."

Abbey knew her friend meant well. "Aha! I see. Amy and Ross are in love. The whole world must be in love. Right?"

Amy chuckled. "Right."

"He's taking you to church tomorrow."

"Right again."

"You have told him what that usually means in Counsel."

"Certainly!"

"Should I pick my bridesmaid's gown now?"

Amy's eyes sparkled mischievously. "Maid of honor,

actually. I thought pale yellow would be nice for a June wedding.''

Abbey propelled herself to the sofa to hug her friend. "Oh, Amy! Congratulations. I'd love to wear yellow at your wedding. For you I'd wear puce polka dots.''

The rest of the afternoon was spent discussing Amy's wedding plans from the morning ceremony to the rose garden reception. Ira arrived home during the recital in time to offer congratulations and a promise to officiate. Ross breezed in to pick up Amy, and a new round of congratulations was initiated. Only their plans to have an engagement dinner with Emil pulled the happy couple away.

Ira and Abbey saw them out. After Ira had closed the door, he smiled at his daughter. "I think Ross is becoming a Counsel convert.''

Abbey linked her arm through his. "It's Amy's pioneering spirit. Ross didn't stand a chance once she'd set her sights on her goal.''

They wandered into the living room, where Abbey turned on the Christmas tree lights. She excused herself to make dinner, refusing Ira's offer of assistance. Ira sat alone, staring at the lights on the tree. His heart bled for her. He was sure that Gabe would not be pleased to have accepted Abbey's help. Gabe had an old-fashioned idea of women. His young wife had fit the pattern, and neither had been given time to grow out of it. Gabe would feel that leaning on a woman for sympathy was a sign of weakness. In his scenario of life, it was only the women who leaned. Ira thought of his own marriage and the warm, enduring courage that Elizabeth Wilson had possessed. He had prayed that Abbey would be given a loving man who matched her as Ira had matched Elizabeth. Now he was forced to watch his daughter's spirit drain away. The death of spiritual love could be more devastating than the loss of someone to physical death. Abbey would have to see Gabe every day, knowing that he had rejected her. Ira prayed fervently that he would be proved wrong.

Monday morning arrived all too soon. Abbey had scheduled visits to several farms that day to see if it would be possible to set up production of Emma Davis's red cider to join next year's line of products.

She and Emma talked over the plans. The older woman was thrilled that Gabe had decided to name the new product "Aunt Emma's Cider." Just as Abbey was leaving, Emma put her arm around her.

"You know that Jordan is courting little Susie Martin. I'd always kind of hope you and Jordan would make a match of it. I want you to know that you'll always be a daughter to me, Abbey Wilson. I don't love you any less because you and my son didn't decide to get hitched. Zeb feels the same way. You don't make yourself scarce around here now, you hear?"

Abbey nodded. "You're all part of my family."

"I just hope Gabe Kendall is good enough for you," Emma stated.

Trying not to look too flabbergasted, Abbey asked, "Emma, where did you get that idea? We're just friends. He's my employer, and that's all."

"Why, the whole town knows he's interested in you, Abbey!"

"That kind of rumor could cost me my job!" Abbey pointed out.

"A lot of people saw you two together up at Campbell's Lodge. Susie saw you and Mr. Kendall visiting your mother's grave last Sunday. We just figured that if you were taking him to your mother's grave, you two were serious."

"Of course," sighed a resigned Abbey.

"Then he helped put up the church nativity scene," Emma added. "Well, you can see how it looks, Abbey dear. It's so perfect. I mean, you were in the city. He came from the city. He owns the cannery. You're a Wilson. We're all real happy for you." Emma was beginning to look worried.

Abbey hugged her and tried to smile. "Let me put it this way. The town appears to know something that we don't. Maybe you could let the ladies know that they're jumping to conclusions. We don't want to embarrass the Kendalls, and I don't think Gabe Kendall has overcome his memories enough to even think about another woman." Abbey made a quick exit.

To Abbey's distress, she found the same rumors and insinuations waiting for her at the other farms she visited. Her only hope was that Gabe's position would keep him from hearing some of the jovial comments and well-meaning advice concerning their relationship.

It was nearly five when Abbey drove into the cannery parking lot to make her report to Gabe. She was just entering the factory when Ross, who was evidently lying in wait for her, grabbed her arm and rushed her out the door.

"Trust me, Abbey. Don't ask questions. Get into your car and meet me at Lesley's. I have her key."

"I have to see Gabe," Abbey protested.

"No, you don't. Not today. Please, Abbey." Ross was so upset that Abbey did as he asked.

When they were finally sitting at Lesley's round table, he blurted out his confession. "You will probably want to kill me, and I don't blame you. I can't tell you how bad I feel about this. You've got to understand that I thought I was helping you and Gabe. I had no idea—''

"Ross, just tell me what has happened. I'm dying of suspense.''

Ross hung his head miserably. "Can I make you some coffee?''

"Ross!" Abbey demanded. "Get to the point.''

He sat back in the chair and avoided her eyes. "You see, the boss was . . . different today. It was like it used to be, before . . . you know. He was more relaxed. Everything was going well at the factory. I was feeling so good because of Amy. I just wanted to share our happiness. Christmas is only a week away.''

"You felt like sharing your happiness.'' Abbey brought him back to the subject at hand.

"Yes. I gave him the news about our wedding. I asked him to be my best man, and he accepted. Then he started teasing me. He was actually teasing me about the responsibilities of being a married man and I . . . I . . .''

"Go on.''

"It's obvious that he loves you, Abbey. I know Amy doesn't think he's good enough for you, but I know him better. I . . . thought . . . I knew him better.''

"Ross, please—what happened?''

"I kidded him back. I've always known how shy Gabe is. I recalled Ann teasing him once about how it took him two years to get up the nerve to ask her to marry him. I just thought if he knew . . . that . . . well . . . Amy said you were in love with him. . . . The whole town . . .''

"You told him the whole town knows that I love him?'' Abbey asked faintly.

"Not exactly. It didn't sound that crude. I just . . . well . . ."

"Oh, Ross!"

The whole story came out in a rush from the repentent Ross. "I sort of suggested that we make it a double wedding. Counsel could make it a town holiday. I advised him to marry you before you were snapped up by someone else. I was only joking, but we all can see how much you and he love each other. Abbey, I thought he was just reluctant to ask, so I tried to spur him on."

"Calm down, Ross. Just tell me what he said before I have to face him."

"His face kind of froze and he said, 'What do you mean, the whole town?' "

"And?" Abbey prodded with a sinking feeling in the pit of her stomach.

"I'm not sure what I said. I babbled about how happy I was to see him so like his old self because of you, and that we all assumed you loved each other. He said, 'It's foolish to make assumptions about the lives of others, Ross. Perhaps your marriage will help you mature in some ways in which you are now deficient.' "

Abbey patted Ross's hand. His imitation of Gabe's deadly tone was uncanny.

"I slunk out with my tail between my legs, but I overheard him tell Lesley on the intercom to have you come to the office as soon as you returned. His voice was not . . . pleasant, Abbey. I explained the situation to Lesley. She gave me her key and said to catch you before you walked into the avalanche."

Abbey stood up. Ross looked stricken. "Abbey, I can't tell you how sorry I am."

"Ross, don't apologize. I've heard the rumors, too. You meant no harm. You see, what none of you seem to realize is that while I love him, he doesn't feel the same way about me. That's why he reacted as he did. Please don't feel so bad. I'd better go back to the factory and talk to him."

"Can't you wait until tomorrow? He'll have time to think about it and mellow a little." Ross grabbed Abbey's hand. "Please, Abbey."

"I promised to report in about the new cider line." Abbey pulled her hand gently from his grasp. "He'll be expecting me. There's no point in putting it off. I'd rather face him now than worry about it all night."

Abbey left the car at home because Ira might need it, and she had no idea how long she would be. It was dusk when she walked the five blocks to the factory. A light snow was beginning to fall. She waved at Millicent, who was looking out of her window as she passed. Several people were leaving work and greeted her on their way home. Lesley was just coming down the stairs and spotted her.

"Abbey! Didn't Ross catch you?"

"He did. I'm going up to face the music right now."

"Oh, Abbey. Don't you think you might want to wait a little while before . . ." Lesley's voice trailed off worriedly.

Abbey shook her head. "It's not something to be put off. However, you might tuck a prayer into the next few minutes for me." Abbey tried to smile to reassure Lesley, but she knew it was a dismal failure. She raced up the stairs, leaving a concerned Lesley behind.

The second floor was silent. Only the shaft of light from Gabe's open door announced his presence. Abbey put her coat and purse in her own office. Then she squared her shoulders, armed herself with her clipboard of facts and figures and marched to that lighted doorway. He was working at his desk on some figures of his own. The overhead light glared down on the dark head; but when he looked up, his eyes were completely devoid of color. With a leaden spirit, Abbey entered the room and closed the door.

Chapter Ten

W e have a problem.'' He waved Abbey to the chair in front of his desk.

Abbey sat down with a sense of déjà vu. It was a repeat of the first day she had met him. His eyes had the same lackluster expression. His voice froze her with the same coldness, as though he were talking to a complete stranger. She girded herself for the onslaught of his criticism. She had the dreadful feeling that she had worked all these months to end up precisely where she had started.

"I don't know if you are aware of the gossip about us." Gabe clipped out each word as though it were repulsive to him. "I wasn't aware of it myself until this afternoon."

Abbey searched his eyes for any spark of feeling, but the washed-out blue did not change.

"It is potentially harmful, both to your reputation and to

the good of the company. I was informed today that it is commonly held by the town that we are . . . involved. I'm sure you can readily see the difficulties.'' He paused, and Abbey felt constrained to speak.

"There is always a great deal of rumormongering in a small town, not to mention a small company." She wished her voice didn't have that dry, tinny sound, but it reflected the recognition of her dreams slowly disintegrating around her.

"It is important that we not give people cause to indulge in that kind of scandal."

Abbey felt bitter when she heard her feelings denigrated by the use of the word "scandal." "It isn't a scandal to be seen with someone in public, Gabe. We're both unmarried adults. Can't you see that it's merely the idle talk of people interested in the doings of others?"

"I don't see it that way."

"I understand." She did. He had found a way to get rid of her. He could not forgive her for having witnessed his tragic vulnerability that night in the attic. They had done nothing wrong. Why was he acting as though their love were a crime? Perhaps, to him, it was.

"I realize that firing you would set the whole town against me. It would be best for everyone concerned if you resigned, Abbey. I'll give you three months' severance pay. After all, I'm mostly to blame. As your employer, I had no right to make advances toward you. Please forgive me. I haven't been thinking straight the last few months."

Abbey unsteadily got to her feet, unable to tear her eyes away from his. "I will do as you wish, of course. But I will not accept that our relationship was in any way dishonorable. I can accept the fact that you don't love me as I love you. I would rather have heard that than these half-truths, Gabe. Perhaps you hide the real truth even from yourself.''

''The truth is that I was temporarily disloyal to the memory of my wife and children,'' Gabe rasped.

''Gabe, you have never been disloyal to their memories. It's just the opposite. You have tried to bury yourself with them. It is not wrong to love another woman after two years. I know you'll never love me the way you loved Ann. I understand that, but you must believe that some-day you will love again. Please don't shut yourself away.''

''Abbey, this is precisely why you must leave. You've interfered in my life from day one. We can't have a good professional relationship, and a personal relationship isn't possible. You must be aware of the attraction I feel for you. However, I have no intention of ever remarrying. This has become an intolerable situation. One of us must go. If I leave, the cannery and the town will suffer. You make the choice.''

He had her, and he knew it. She couldn't let the town down. Right now he was far more important to Counsel than she was. Abbey laid her clipboard on the desk in front of him.

''Here are the figures for the new cider line. I'll work with Ross and Lesley tomorrow so that they'll be familiar with my job. I'll be gone by Wednesday, if that's accepta-ble.''

He nodded, studying the papers on his desk to avoid looking at her.

Quietly Abbey left him still staring at the papers. She returned to her office, retrieved her coat, then numbly stumbled down the stairs, through the lobby and out the door. The few flakes had escalated into a blizzard. She was thankful for the snow, for the tears running down her face would be disguised by the heavy flakes. Christmas was a cruel time to lose her love and her job. Abbey's cup of misery was full enough; she didn't need the sound of children's voices singing carols on the corner to serve as a counterrhythm to her despair.

Over and over, a lament ran through her mind: "I will never see him again. After tomorrow, I will never see him again." That theme seemed to dominate her symphony of desolation. The sub-themes of finding work, anxiety about helping her father and the mortification of being rejected in front of the whole town by the man she loved ran poor seconds to the fact that she would not even be allowed to be near him.

She didn't remember going up the steps of the house or opening the door. All at once she was standing in the living room with her clothes dripping on the old rug as she faced Ira, Lesley, Amy and Ross, who had been anxiously waiting for news. She tried to pull the shreds of her shattered dignity about her to comfort the others. This time her compassion eluded her grasp. She couldn't think of one single helpful thing to say. Her face revealed the whole story to them.

"I'm sorry," she faltered.

Ross was galvanized into action, nearly tripping over Ira in order to take Abbey's wet coat. Lesley and Amy rescued her from the well-meaning attentions of the men and hurried her upstairs and into a hot bath. Amy tucked her into bed with a hot-water bottle while Lesley brought up hot food. Neither asked for particulars or bothered her with empty chatter.

After sipping some soup, Abbey wearily informed Lesley that she and Ross would have to take over her job until a replacement could be found.

"He only gave you one day's notice?" Lesley was aghast.

"No. I set the time," Abbey explained. "I could see he wanted me out as soon as possible. He offered me severance pay."

"Hmmmmph!" Lesley looked meaningfully at Amy over Abbey's head, and they went downstairs to join the men.

The constant murmur of voices below her did not penetrate Abbey's exhaustion. She would face the problem tomorrow. "In Your hands . . ." She offered a brief prayer before she fell into a deep, dreamless sleep.

The next morning Ross picked up Abbey and drove her to the cannery. They immediately went to her office, but not before Abbey noticed that Gabe's office was empty. He had not come to work, in order to avoid seeing her. Abbey felt a small stab of anguish pierce her sadness. She would never see him again.

"You're late for work," Ralph commented to his son over the breakfast table.

"I thought I'd take the day off." Gabe had dark shadows under his eyes, but his father had no pity for him.

"Is it true that you fired Abbey Wilson?"

"She resigned."

Ralph gave Gabe a sharp look. "Because you asked her to, in order to save your stupid Kendall pride."

Gabe responded to the unexpected attack. "The gossip in the town was detrimental to her reputation and to the cannery. She felt it was the best thing to do under the circumstances."

"Balderdash! You found her presence uncomfortable because you felt guilty about loving her. You couldn't bear to have someone around who knew you as well as she did, so you got rid of her."

"That's not true, Dad! You don't understand."

"I understand you and your dense Welsh stubbornness very well, Gabriel Kendall. You should know yourself as well as I know you. God has given you a second chance at happiness, and you're throwing it away because you are still mad at Him. You're like a bad little boy who throws away cake because he wants pie."

Gabe answered levelly, "That's unfair. You're distressing yourself over nothing. You're going to work yourself up into another stroke."

"At least I can work myself up into something. That's better than being a zombie for the rest of my life."

Gabe got up from the table to address his father in a carefully controlled voice. "This is getting us nowhere. I had to decide what is best for me and the factory."

"Well, your decision is disastrous!" shouted Ralph.

"To whom?" snapped Gabe.

"To you, to the town, to the cannery, to the future," Ralph retorted.

"Abbey Wilson pitied me. Pity is not love," Gabe stated flatly.

"If you believe that it was pity she felt for you, Gabe, you are truly blind. Abbey Wilson loves you. How else could she have stood all of the garbage you dumped on her?"

"I have no intention of marrying again. I'm not going to throw away the memory of my family, even if you're willing to do so!" Two angry spots of red stained his cheekbones. Suddenly he realized what was happening. "We'll talk about this some other time, Dad. This is upsetting you."

"What's upsetting me," growled Ralph, "is your obtuseness. Do you think I love Ann less because I could love Abbey as your wife, too? Ann is dead, Gabe. The twins are gone. But you're alive. Don't let your pride get in the way of your heart."

Gabe left the room without a word. Ralph heard the car engine and knew his son had left. He prayed that he had not just lost his son with his harsh words. Ira had warned him not to make matters worse by castigating Gabe, but Ralph firmly believed in the truth that makes men free. If he couldn't feel free to tell the truth to Gabe, they had no relationship left.

By midmorning the word had gotten around. The clerks and secretaries from the second floor had informed the people on the first floor. After lunch the entire factory knew that Abbey was leaving her job. Everyone found an excuse to visit the second floor and say a kind word to her. The afternoon was extremely difficult, but Abbey finally felt that Lesley and Ross had the information they needed to carry on.

Ross shook his head dolefully. "There's no way I can do all of this, even with Lesley's help. Some of these projects

are going to have to wait a long time before I get to them."
He began carrying Abbey's three boxes of personal belongings to his car.

Abbey handed her philodendron to Lesley. "It's used to this place," she reflected sadly. "It flourished here, even if I didn't." Abbey followed Ross out to the parking lot, where she was stopped by old Mr. Petty, the night watchman.

"I came early to catch you." He panted. "My granddaughter in accounting told me you got fired. I just wanted you to know that I think it's a real shame. You were so nice to bring me those treats after the party. Kendall's making a terrible mistake."

Abbey let the old man pump her hand sorrowfully. "I resigned, Mr. Petty."

"Yeah, well, of course you have to say that, but I just figured he got jealous of how much influence you Wilsons have in this town."

"Oh no, Mr. Petty. That's not at all true. Please don't think that. The job just wasn't working out, that's all."

"You're a nice young lady, Miss Wilson, but the town has pretty well nailed down who's at fault. I'm not saying that Mr. Kendall isn't a decent enough fella. He's just not too smart about some things. He'll be real sorry when you're gone."

Abbey tried to clarify the situation with the watchman, but soon realized that she was wasting her time. The town had decided the truth, and that was that. She knew that he was merely repeating what he had heard. Nothing was going to change the mind of the old man, or the minds of those who had told him the story. She got into Ross's car and sighed hopelessly. How was she going to straighten out this mess so that Gabe didn't suffer? She asked Ross for advice.

"Let him suffer." Ross was angry at Gabe and at himself for having precipitated this disaster. "Mr. Petty is right. Gabe was so busy seeing you as a woman, he didn't realize how much work you were doing. He'll find out soon enough."

"He's endured enough."

"No. I believed that, too." Ross stared ahead as he maneuvered the car through the parking lot gates. "I felt sorry for him until he hurt you. He can't keep taking his misery out on other people. Amy was right about him; I was wrong. She said that he'd never be able to love you because he was too immersed in his own self-pity. I should have listened to her. I might have been able to spare you this if I had. Amy always tells it like it is. She was right about me, and she's right about Gabe."

"I love Amy. She sees you clearly and loves you, Ross. But, Ross, you see, I love Gabe."

"Aw, Abbey. It's so unfair. Why didn't I keep my big mouth shut?"

"It would have happened whether you had spoken or not. Believe me, Ross. None of this is your fault."

Amy had picked up dinner at Mama Scarpino's and had it waiting on the table when they arrived. She greeted them with messages. "Ira is over at Lesley's. Mama sends her love and says that she'll put hot peppers in Gabe Kendall's pasta the next time he eats there. I may not be a good cook, but I'm a wonderful delivery girl. Get it while it's hot!"

"The news has spread through the town like wildfire.

Mr. Petty stopped us in the parking lot," Abbey murmured as she glumly fell into a chair.

"The Davises, the Baileys, the Paynes and Susie Martin have already called." Amy handed the garlic bread to Ross. "It will be rough for a few days, but everyone is on your side."

"That's just what I don't want! I don't want trouble for Gabe or the cannery." Abbey couldn't eat.

"Eat, or you are going to have trouble with me," threatened Amy.

"Honestly, you two don't have to baby-sit me," Abbey protested. "I'm perfectly fine, everything considered."

"Eat!" commanded Ross and Amy together. Abbey obeyed to keep the peace.

After supper, Ross and Amy left to do some last-minute shopping. Abbey decided to wrap some of her presents and put them under the tree. She refused to feel sorry for herself. Determinedly she put a stack of carols on her elderly record player and wrapped the gifts. As she was putting them under the tree, she noticed the light on in the kitchen. She started in to say hello to her father and stopped. Ira was sitting at the table with Lesley. They were holding hands and sipping cocoa. Lesley's complexion was a delicate shade of pink and her eyes were luminescent as she fondly gazed into Ira's face. Abbey tiptoed backward so she wouldn't disturb them.

She smiled to herself in the dimness of the hall. For a moment she was able to forget her own unhappiness as she softly retraced her steps. One problem had been solved. The only thing that had held her in Counsel was her concern for her father, and she now knew that the Lord had sent someone to keep an eye on him. Abbey went to her desk and pulled out her battered typewriter. She began the rough draft of a letter to Chicago asking for a job with her old firm. Even if she had to start at the bottom again, she knew she could work her way up. After proofing the finished copy, she tucked it into an envelope, deciding to mail it immediately before she began to vacillate.

She made a great deal of unnecessary noise clattering down the stairs. When she looked in the kitchen, Lesley was drinking cold cocoa and her eyes had a telltale brightness. Abbey told Ira and Lesley of her plan to return to Chicago.

"I know Dad feels I am running his life too much," she joked. "I'm fairly sure I'll be rehired in some capacity. By the time I come home for a visit, the town will have gotten over this nine days' wonder and everything will be back to normal."

Lesley said with regret, "No one will do that job as well as you, Abbey. It's all so unfortunate."

Ira patted Lesley's hand. "I don't know why you two have so much trouble leaving things in the Lord's hands. You must have faith."

"It's my meddling that got me into trouble in the first place," admitted Abbey. "I'm going to take Neb out and mail this letter tonight. We could both use some exercise." Neb lifted his head from Ira's foot inquiringly. "Come on, Neb. Let's go out."

The snowstorm had ended and Neb cavorted about in circles, throwing snow all over Abbey. They mailed the letter and admired Main Street dressed in its costume of Christmas lights and tinsel. It was after store hours, so the streets were deserted. Only one car was on the road, wending its lonely way toward the outskirts of town, away from the factory. So Gabe had worked this evening, thought Abbey. He probably felt he had to make up for the time he'd lost today.

Abbey held her ground with Neb at her side. She knew he saw her. He couldn't have missed her, standing under the streetlight in her red jacket. The car passed by without changing speed. The dark profile in the car was averted from her.

"Oh, Gabe," Abbey felt a sob catch in her throat. "Couldn't you even look at me?"

Despondently she turned and headed home. Sensing her anguish, Neb walked at her side, bumping her occasionally with his head to show his sympathy. She did not look back to see that the car had paused before turning onto the country road.

Gabe gazed into his rearview mirror as he watched the dejected figure in the red coat slowly disappear from view. He almost turned the car around to catch up with her, but his courage failed him. He must live with his decision. It would be cruel to open the lines of communication with Abbey once more. Their time was over. He pushed on the accelerator and sped away from the sight of the slight figure. But his mind could not escape his memories as easily.

The day had begun badly for Gabe. He had awakened with a feeling of depression. His father's rough advice had driven him from the house, but he had spent the day away from the cannery because he couldn't bear to witness Abbey's departure. He had driven to Des Moines to pick up some presents for his father, but found he was not in any mood for the task. After a dismal lunch at a shopping center, he'd returned to the cannery to find that everyone had gone for the day. He tortured himself by looking in

Abbey's empty office. Going into his own office, he found her notes written in her round backhand still on his desk. He accomplished nothing, but punished himself by sticking at it for several hours. When he called his father, Ralph informed him that Ira had helped him to bed, so Gabe needn't bother to come home early. Then he had walked down to Mama's for a solitary supper and received a cool reception from the usually volatile Scarpinos. On the way back he was accosted by Millicent Shriers.

The elderly lady had thrown on a heavy shawl and hailed him from her doorstep. Like a small boy with his hand caught in the cookie jar, he approached the little white-haired lady warily. Much to his relief, she handed him a paper plate full of molasses bars.

"I thought you might like some homemade goodies, it being so close to Christmas." She regarded him with sharp black eyes. "You look like you could use some treats to pep you up."

"Thank you." Gabe kissed her parchment cheek.

"Come in, young man."

He hesitated. Millicent was one of the Wilsons' good friends.

"I won't bite you," she promised. "You seem to be hurting yourself enough without me giving you the back of my tongue, although you probably deserve it."

She solved the problem by fastening a tiny hand on his sleeve and tugging him into the house. She led him to the big kitchen, pushed him into a chair and poured him a large mug of coffee.

Gabe ran his hand over the polished oak of the trestle table. "This is a fine piece of workmanship."

She set a large piece of pumpkin pie in front of him and

sat down. "My first husband, Mike, made it with his own hands. He was a carpenter. He was killed when the old granary burned in '32. I thought my life was over back then."

"You've been widowed a long time."

"Nope. I married Charlie in '35. We were married over thirty years. He was a farmer. He died of a stroke in '69. That's when I moved back into this house that Charlie had built for me and sold the farm." She got up to pour more coffee.

Gabe looked at her and prepared to take his medicine. He had a good idea why she had asked him in. "You were lucky to have found two good men."

She gave him a wicked smile. "I would have found a third good man if there had been one old enough and available, young man. Don't look at me like that. I believe in love and marriage. Mike wouldn't have wanted me to stop living just because he had. He really loved me. People who love you want you to be happy." She poked a bony forefinger into his arm. "I'm sorry your marriage wasn't so good."

"I had a wonderful marriage." Gabe scowled. "We loved each other very much."

"That's odd," ruminated Millicent. "Usually when a man has had a good marriage, he's looking for a second wife after a while. He has faith in love because of the first one, you see."

"I'm sure that people want to believe that when they marry a second time," grated Gabe. "It salves their consciences about betraying their former spouses."

"Nonsense. I'd have been very angry with Mike or

Charlie if I'd died and they'd given up on marriage. It would have made me look bad. Didn't your wife love you?''

"Of course she did!"

"Oh?" Millicent looked skeptical.

"Love is supposed to be eternal."

"It is, but no one says you can't love more than once. You were jealous of your wife, I take it."

"What?"

"If you had died, wouldn't you have wanted her to marry again? Would you have expected her to spend the rest of her life alone? Kind of mean-spirited, don't you think?''

"I . . ." Gabe was dumbfounded. He had never considered that possibility. What if he had died instead of Ann? Would he have wanted his young wife to live out her life alone? He shook his head. Of course not. He would have expected her to find a good husband and raise the children. He loved them, and he would have wanted them to be happy. Gabe focused on the small wrinkled face in front of him.

Millicent gave him a knowing smile. "I figured you hadn't thought it out too good.''

Gabe had gone back to the cannery from Millicent's in a daze. When he had spotted Abbey standing on the corner, he had almost stopped to talk to her about his new thoughts, but he'd felt it was unfair. He had resisted the temptation to go to her and explain his confusion. He wasn't going to lay any more problems at her feet; he had hurt her enough. As he drove into his own drive, he stopped the car and looked up at the stars. He had come to a conclusion.

It was too much for him to sort out. Abbey believed God

did everything for a reason. It was time to trust Him. Gabe lifted his face to the starry sky. "It's in Your hands, Lord."

Abbey spent the remaining days before Christmas Eve working at the church with the other volunteers. She delivered baskets to the ill, indigent and homebound. She helped with a luncheon for the golden-agers and hosted the men's club Christmas party at the social center. Through it all, she held her head up high under the concerned looks and remarks of the townspeople.

Ross reported the situation from the cannery. "It's really weird," he said. "I don't see how Gabe stands it. We've had dozens of complaints from the subcontractors because we can't keep to your schedule, Abbey. I expected him to jump all over me, but he doesn't. When Zeb Davis told him that he was a real fool to let you go, I thought we'd really have fireworks. He just looked at Zeb and shook his head."

"Well," commented Amy, "the truth is the truth. What could he say?"

"He's smart enough to wait it out," Abbey reasoned. "It'll all be over as soon as I leave town. Everyone will forget."

"Lesley nearly had a fit today when she couldn't find the philodendron you gave her. She had us looking for it all over the office. We were positive he had thrown it out just to be rid of any reminders. Guess where we found it!"

Abbey tried not to sound too interested. "Where?"

"In his office, on the windowsill. He said it needed more sun. I thought Lesley would faint. He's never cared about plants before."

Amy smiled a secret smile. "Interesting."

"No one knows what to expect," sputtered Ross. "We all tiptoed around waiting for something to happen. Even old Mr. Petty gave him a piece of his mind. He told Gabe it wasn't too late to fix up a mistake. The payroll manager asked him if Abbey should receive the Christmas bonus and the ham. He just blinked and told her to go ahead and send the ham to the house.

"The real cropper came when they delivered all those poinsettias to the office that Abbey had ordered for the subcontractors. The Payne boy refused to deliver them to the farms. He said that his mother only told him to deliver them to the office. We were knee-deep in poinsettias. Even then Gabe didn't get mad. He just took Abbey's list and borrowed a truck from the foreman. Then he had some of the men carry the plants to the truck. After that he disappeared for the rest of the day."

"I had forgotten about those poinsettias," murmured Abbey.

"He must be having some kind of breakdown," stated Ross.

"He'll have to deliver those plants to the farms himself," Amy mused. "I'd love to be there when Emma Davis gets a hold of him."

Lesley reported that Gabe was spending even longer hours in the cannery. "He looks thinner than ever," she informed Abbey while they were doing some Christmas baking. Ira was the self-appointed official taster. "Did I tell you that the entire assembly line signed a petition asking to have you reinstated? Gabe merely accepted it from the foreman, went into his office and shut the door."

"This has got to stop." Abbey brushed the flour from her

hands. "It's become persecution. He has the right to hire and fire whoever he wishes. If this keeps up, the Kendalls are going to be driven out of Counsel."

"No," said Ira, "Ralph said he'd stay and run the cannery if Gabe decided to leave."

"Dad! You've got to do something! Tell everyone to lay off. They'll listen to you."

Ira licked his fingers thoughtfully and took another cookie. "He is only getting his just deserts."

"What about revenge belonging to the Lord?" Abbey fixed her father with a grim eye.

"There is a difference between revenge and just retribution," Ira said.

"Dad!"

"Can I have another cookie?" Ira avoided her eyes completely. "If it concerns you so much and since tomorrow is Christmas Eve, I will have a word with a few people."

Abbey trusted Ira and did not bring up the topic again. The next morning she helped decorate the church with fresh pine boughs and poinsettias. She put the old Bible on its stand with a red ribbon marking the Christmas story for midnight services. It had been a trying morning because apparently some of the ladies hadn't gotten the word yet. They would be whispering in corners and stopped whenever Abbey came within hearing distance. Sometimes she wished that Counsel weren't quite such a small town.

All afternoon, people dropped by with food and gifts for Ira and Abbey. Amy delivered her gifts along with Ross's, but refused to stay for coffee.

"I'll see you tonight at services. What are you wearing?"

Abbey laughed. "My heart on my sleeve for the whole world to see. I have no idea, Amy."

Amy said sternly, "Take my advice. You don't want the town to feel sorry for you and say you've already started to let yourself go, do you? Wear something pretty and go with all your flags flying, Abbey. Promise?"

Impatient with the subject, Abbey agreed to wear the emerald green dress that she had bought when she thought the company was still going to have a Christmas party. Amy approved the choice and went off with a jaunty wave.

Abbey set the table for an early supper. Her father liked to spend some time reviewing his sermon and meditating before a service. As it turned out, Ira didn't return home on time and the meal was nearly ruined.

"I'm sorry. I had an emergency meeting." He quickly ate his overdone dinner and disappeared into his study. Abbey assumed that he had done some last-minute shopping for her. His shopping was always rushed because the church had to come first in his priorities.

Abbey dressed early because she expected some late visitors on Christmas Eve, but strangely, no one came. She supposed that everyone felt that she preferred to be alone. She shrugged philosophically and stopped to check her reflection in the mirror. Her face had thinned over the last few weeks, and her eyes seemed enormous in the glass. The emerald green of the dress made her eyes and hair appear darker than usual and gave her skin a pearly glow.

They were due to leave for service in half an hour. Lesley would be arriving soon to join them. The house seemed unusually quiet. While Abbey waited, she let Sheba in and Neb out the back door for a run. It was a magical night. The snow was a glistening white mantle on the ground, and the stars shone like diamonds in the black velvet sky. She had loved Christmas Eve as a child. How special this night had always been to her.

"I will not think of anything tonight except the birth we celebrate," she vowed. "The Lord doesn't make mistakes. He knows what is best." She heard Ira's voice calling her as she stepped back into the warmth of the kitchen.

"It's time to go," Ira said. "Get your coat."

"Dad, what's the hurry?" Abbey asked in surprise. "It's still early. Lesley isn't here yet."

"I saw her coming up the walk," insisted Ira. "Put on your coat. We don't want to be late."

The doorbell rang. "See? There she is. Let's go."

It must be love, thought Abbey humorously as she threw her coat on. She stepped out the door onto the porch and froze.

It looked to Abbey as though the entire town had congregated in a semicircle on her front yard. She looked at the group in astonishment. She saw Amy and her father with Ross. The entire Scarpino family was there with Millicent Shriers. The Payne family was waving and smiling at her. The foreman of the cannery line and his family, the clerks and secretaries, the farmers and carpenters, including the Davis and Bailey families, were there. Ira and Lesley each took one of Abbey's hands and led her to the edge of the porch.

Through the crowd came a tall, broad-shouldered figure that she recognized immediately. Gabe Kendall pushed his father's wheelchair to the front of the crowd and stepped forward until he was in the center of the half-circle. He faced Abbey directly.

"Abbey Wilson, I'm here to apologize for firing you. I find that I can't do without you in my work, or in my life. Would you accept my apology, Abbey, and accept me, too. Think it over carefully. A lifetime is a long time. I have brought these witnesses so you can't change your mind should you decide to accept me."

Abbey would have collapsed if Ira and Lesley had not been holding her up. Her heart nearly stopped. How had this intensely private man found the humility to apologize, propose and wait for an answer in front of an entire town who had treated him like a pariah for the past week? If ever Abbey had doubted his love, she couldn't now, knowing the courage it must have taken for him to do this.

She ran down the porch steps and threw herself into his arms. He gripped her tightly and then gently pushed her from him in order to take a sparkling object out of his pocket. He held up the ring and the crowd roared its approval as they had when she had run to him. He placed it securely on her finger and bent down to kiss her.

"How did you know I'd say yes?" Abbey whispered.

He whispered back, "You said the Lord never makes mistakes. The whole town was praying for us. How could I go wrong?"

Over the cheering throng came the pealing of the church bells calling them to Christmas services. Everyone congratulated the happy couple on their way to the church.

Amy murmured into Abbey's ear, "I knew he loved you when he usurped that ridiculous philodendron. Only a man in love would do that."

At last Abbey and Gabe followed the congregation into the church. The joyous ringing of the bells ushered them in, the same bells that would announce the celebration of their wedding day.

"Have I told you that I love you?" asked Gabe softly.

"No, but you'll get a lot of chances to make up for it," Abbey assured him. "You have always known that I loved you, now and forever. And forever can be a very long time."

If you enjoyed
this book...

then you're sure to enjoy our Silhouette Inspirations Home Subscription Service℠! You'll receive two new Silhouette Inspirations™ novels—written by Christian women, *for* Christian women—each month, as soon as they are published.

Examine your books for 15 days, free.

Return the coupon below, and we'll send you two Silhouette Inspirations novels to examine for 15 days, free. If you're as pleased with your books as we think you will be, just pay the enclosed invoice. Then every month, you'll receive two tender love stories—and you'll never pay any postage, handling or packing costs. If not delighted, simply return the books and owe nothing. There is no minimum number of books to buy, and you may cancel at any time.

Return the coupon today...and soon you'll share the joy of Silhouette Inspirations. Love stories that touch the heart as well as the soul.